Love Without Borders

by

NADEEM AKBAR

First published in India in 2016 by:
Nadeem Akbar

Copyright © 2016 Nadeem Akbar

Print Book ISBN: 9789384439736
eBook ISBN: 9789384439743

Nadeem Akbar asserts the moral right to be identified as the author of this work.

Typeset by Ram Das Lal, New Delhi (NCR)

Publishing facilitation: AuthorsUpFront

Cover design: Neena Gupta

Contents

*Dedicated to love, peace and
a world without borders*

Chapter One

⟡

Shahnawaz was feeling restless again. He gazed out of the window of his apartment on the 42nd floor. A crystalline Manhattan spread out below him – the East River, and beyond, Queens. He found himself looking out often – there was solace in the beautiful view. Dusk turned to dark, and the lights of the city blinked on. The shimmering grey water of the East River had been his companion many a lonely night, the lights along the Triborough Bridge a sentinel guarding against the world beyond the city.

But tonight, there was no solace. His thoughts raced along paths of what might have been. If the rocket had not hit the house…. If he had been there to do something…… If his wife and daughter had not been home alone…… Why his family? He was a good man; he had done good deeds. He did not deserve such punishment from God. These thoughts made him question his faith sometimes. Anger seethed in him.

* * *

He was stationed at Mazar-i-Shareef Air Base when he was told that his father's house near Kabul had been destroyed. At first, he could not speak. The moment froze, became an eternity.

On the plane home, he felt as if he were moving in slow motion. His brother Rubnawaz and his father Allahnawaz were waiting at the airport.

"*Assalam-o-alaikum*," he said. "Everyone is all right?"

"Come home and we will talk," his father replied, not meeting his eyes.

On the drive home, he thought, *Why is my father not saying anything? Maybe mother is injured.* He dared not ask. He convinced himself that his wife and daughter had escaped harm. They were in the prime of life. It was not possible.

They reached their destination in silence. A canopy for prayers had been hastily erected in the garden, partly obscuring his view. As the car pulled around it, what he saw was so traumatic that for a split second, he did not believe it. The house was in ruins, much of the roof caved in. In the rooms with ceilings intact, windows and doors had been blown out. One door still hung by a single hinge, leaning out at a crazy angle. There were people everywhere.

He leapt from the car and ran towards the house. A group of women parted to let him through. They had washed and wrapped three bodies in preparation for the funeral.

The bodies lay on litters, swathed in white cloth. One was his mother; the second was his wife. He could hardly bear to look at the third, small form. When he did, he saw his daughter sleeping peacefully, a hint of a smile on her pudgy face. But she was not asleep.

"Oh! My God! No! No!"

Later, this scene from the world he'd left behind replayed itself in his mind, over and over: He, the eldest son of a proud Afghan family, sobbing helplessly, hugging his small lifeless daughter to his chest, rocking back and forth. The memory involved all his senses. He could smell the charred embers of his house; feel the weight of the child in his arms; hear his own anguished moans.

"Control yourself, Shahnawaz," scolded Allahnawaz. His face was stern. "We will find out who did this. We will not rest till we take revenge. This I promise you."

"But Baba, why are we being targeted?" he asked, rubbing his cheeks hard with his fingers, as if to erase the tears.

"The truth will reveal itself," replied his father. "And soon, our enemies will know that they have transgressed against the wrong people."

"What enemies? We have no enemies," Shahnawaz insisted. As if there were no evidence.

"No. This is definitely the work of an enemy."

* * *

When he had been assigned to Mazar-i-Shareef, his wife and daughter had remained with his parents. He missed them terribly. He qualified for family accommodations as an officer, but had to wait his turn. Finally, his name reached the top of the list and he was allotted a small apartment. He had applied for ten days leave to help with arrangements and deliver the good news in person.

Then, the rocket attack. He never got to tell his beloved Sara. She never knew.

* * *

The remaining rooms in the house were uninhabitable. A neighbor, Wahab Khan, offered his father shelter.

"Please, Allahnawaz, come and live at my house until you find a place to rent. Bring your sons with you."

"No, thank you, we will manage." His Afghan pride did not allow him to accept help easily.

"I would be hurt, should you reject my offer."

"You leave me no choice, then," Allahnawaz agreed. Briefly, his eyes glistened. "We will come after the funeral."

A simple prayer was said under the canopy, and relatives gathered to carry the deceased on litters to the graveyard. So many mourners, gathering quickly for those so deeply loved.

Then the burial, the shrouded bodies laid directly in the ground. People were walking away, talking quietly, when Shahnawaz noticed a man at the edge of the crowd. He had seen the stranger earlier, staring at him. Like many of the guests, he wore a gun. Then, the stranger reached for his weapon, and began firing. Shahnawaz drew his own gun – a reflex – and returned but stopped almost immediately, fearful of injuring the mourners. His father, walking beside him, stopped suddenly, as if he had run into an invisible wall.

Other men were shouting and running. The attacker disappeared over a hill. Shahnawaz heard a screech of tires and the sound of a car speeding off. He saw his relatives stop as they reached the hilltop, shaking their heads and lowering their weapons. He felt a weight against his feet and looked down. It was his father.

Allahnawaz lay on the ground oddly. The old man's eyes were blank, wide open. Blood pooled around him, soaking the grass. Shahnawaz had seen such deaths before.

He crouched down between the graves beside the older man, hugging his own shoulders as if to hold himself together. His whole body was shaking. This time, there were no tears. A hand jerked at his arm urgently.

"Come quickly, brother." It was Rubnawaz. "There may be others nearby."

"Others?" said Shahnawaz. He steadied himself, and rose. Friends and relatives helped with his father's body, carrying him from the graveyard on the litter that had brought his wife there just a short time earlier, hurrying – eyes darting to every side, anticipating danger, not knowing where to turn.

* * *

Wahab Khan joined the brothers in the guest room he had offered them. They rose when he entered.

"There are things I must discuss with you both."

"What is it, sir?" Shahnawaz asked.

"I have received important information about the attack on your father's house, and the identity of the killers."

"Tell us who they are, sir." Rubnawaz said, clenching his fists until the nails dug into his palms. His voice choked with anger. "We will find them and kill them. Every last one."

"Alas, it is not that simple, my friend. You must leave Afghanistan today, cross the border into Pakistan. Your life is in immediate danger."

"We are not cowards, sir," said Shahnawaz. "We will not run."

"This is no time to argue, Shahwanaz. Be reasonable. They mean to kill you. No doubt your brother too. You must go as soon as we can arrange it. They will not attack this house – they do not want me as an enemy. But the moment you leave these walls, you are no longer under my protection. You will surely die."

"Sir, my father has just been murdered. I buried my mother and daughter and wife just a few hours ago. How can you ask this of me?"

"I know how you must feel. But it is necessary to wait and plan. If you are killed tomorrow, what good will that do? How then will you take your revenge?"

Wahab Khan's words were calm but firm, filled with the grave realities of the situation.

"But my father's funeral…," Shahnawaz continued.

"I will arrange the funeral. It is the least I can do for my friend. Your father is gone. I cannot help him now," the older man's voice rose. "But I will not let his sons die."

Shahnawaz was not convinced. His mind buzzed with questions. His mobile phone rang and he answered. It was his trusted friend and colleague in the Air Force.

"Shahnawaz? This is Jamshed. "*Inna lillahi wa inna ilayhi raji'un.* I am sorry for your loss."

"Thank you, my friend," said Shahnawaz. "And how are you?" he added automatically, as if nothing had happened.

"Fine, fine," replied Jamshed, dismissing the pleasantry. "But you are not. You are in danger."

"What are you telling me? Uncle Wahab says the same thing."

"This is why. Remember the attack on that Taliban hideout? With Commander Akbar and the NATO forces?"

"Of course."

"You killed innocent people that day."

"I need no reminding, Jamshed. I will never excuse myself for what happened."

"Bad intelligence, my friend. It was not your fault. But the Tabani do not see it that way. They lost young men that day – women and children too. Now, they've found out who flew those copters. They want revenge."

Shahnawaz was shocked. He held no malice toward the Tabani; he had been carrying out orders.

"Tariq Tabani's son Saleem was among them. At the funeral, he swore revenge." Jamshed said this matter-of-factly. The reaction was expected. Honor demanded it.

"How did you find out?" Shahnawaz asked. His throat was dry, and there was a throbbing in his temples.

"I was on leave, remember? Attending my cousin's wedding?"

"Yes."

"A relative asked if I knew you. When I told him that I was your friend, he said you were in grave danger, that the Tabani wanted you dead. He told me to alert you. But there was no time. And now, your family is gone."

"Tell me the names of my enemies. I will be grateful to you."

"That I will not do. My aim is to save you, not to send you on a sure path to Allah. You and your brother must get out of Afghanistan. You know why you are still alive?

"Why?" Shahnawaz asked irritably. It didn't matter. His own life meant nothing to him now.

"They thought you would be home when they attacked. When they found you had not been there, they came to kill you at the graveyard. Your father was collateral damage. They will try again. Soon."

"So what should I do?"

"You must leave Afghanistan. Don't return to the base at

all. They already went after Akbar, but did not succeed. He will recover."

"I will not run," repeated Shahnawaz, still obstinate.

"Go, Shahnawaz. Take your brother and protect him. But keep in touch. We are working to gather elders for a *Jirga*. If they decide in your favor, the Tabani will accept compensation for their losses. Then it will be safe to return."

"What about my post?"

"I will make sure that your leave is extended till we reach a settlement."

Jamshed was certain, but Shahnawaz's mind was in turmoil. Thoughts deadly as bullets ricocheted around his brain. He struggled to believe his whole family was gone. He cursed his inability to protect them. And now, it was clear they had died in his place. The shot that killed his father had been meant for him. How could he do nothing?

"For God's sake, man, I cannot run away. I must take my revenge; and if, in doing so, I get killed too, that is all right. How can I live with the knowledge that I saved myself without avenging my family?"

"No, Shahnawaz, it will not be all right. Consider your situation – you are on your own now. Rubnawaz is hardly a man. You must take time and think calmly. Your enemies are strong and they plan ahead. If you are killed, their victory will be total. Save yourself and learn more about them. Plan your revenge, or you will be annihilated. Then, your father's soul will curse you for not keeping yourself alive to make your enemies pay."

* * *

Wahab Khan, as a good friend and neighbor, made

arrangements for Allahnawaz's burial, a safe distance from the other family graves. He forbade the brothers to attend.

Shahnawaz was frustrated, agitated. Anger burned within him. He paced up and down the garden, unable to stay still. He felt a prisoner in Wahab Khan's house.

He went over the options with Raby, whose passion and anger almost exceeded his own; he spoke to Wahab Khan again and again. But his host was adamant, and the wisdom of the older man prevailed. Shahnawaz agreed to play the waiting game, though every instinct fought against it. *Then*, he convinced himself, *the Tabani will be lulled into a sense of security. Then I will strike.*

Wahab Khan made arrangements to finalize an escape. Time dragged on.

* * *

One black night, Shahnawaz could stand it no longer. As dawn approached and the horizon lightened, he slipped from the compound and made his way to his father's grave, a mile and a half from the ruined house that had once sheltered his family and his future. He knew his actions might affront his gracious host. But he had to make peace with his father.

At the grave, he knelt and wept again, begging forgiveness – for letting Allahnawaz be buried so far from his family; for causing his death; for having to flee the country with his brother.

"These were not my choices, Baba," Shahnawaz said, tears stinging his eyes and falling onto the wreaths his father's admirers had placed around the grave. The flowers had already withered. "But I swear, once Raby is settled, and I am free to make my own decisions, the Tabani will weep over the bodies of those they love as I weep now over yours."

The sun was rising fast. He could not bear to go. But he could not bear to stay either. Besides, Raby was waiting and daylight brought danger. Reluctantly, he said his goodbyes and returned to Wahab Khan's house. The grief inside him was astonishingly physical – as if something had been gouged from his very being.

When he arrived, Rubnawaz was already awake, his eyes full of questions. Shahnawaz stared at the wall beyond him. He could not meet his brother's gaze.

"I am sorry, Raby," he said mechanically. "I had to make my heartfelt apologies to Baba. It is I who have brought destruction to this family."

"No, no, brother. You did your duty as an officer in the attack. You did not set out to kill innocents. You did not know the Tabani would suffer." Raby paused. "But they will pay," he added, gritting his teeth. "They are murderers."

* * *

The memories blurred; but the lights on the Triborough Bridge burned clearly. Today was the ninth of December. He had married Sara on this very day, just ten years ago. He stepped back, gazing at his reflection in the window, and for a second, saw her face, her wide eyes lost and sad. He had been staring through the glass for hours, the memories raging. The splendid view seemed distant and alien; the walls of his apartment pressed in. He could not stay here grieving any longer. He needed life around him, reassurance that he was not alone – a restaurant, perhaps, surrounded by strangers. Maybe the irrepressible energy of his adopted city would be a tonic. He put on a camel's hair coat and a grey cashmere scarf and walked out, into the biting wind.

In his favorite cafe, he took his usual seat at a corner table near a window. Outside, the streets were chill and grey. It started to rain, the drops streaking the glass. New Yorkers, as always, were unperturbed. People hurried by, light glistening on their wet umbrellas. The street lights sparkled. Always, there was a spirit of excitement in this city.

The restaurant filled up quickly. There were three vacant seats at Shahnawaz's table. He looked up to find the waiter standing beside him.

"Sorry to bother you, sir. We are so busy tonight. Would you mind sharing?"

The bubble burst. He had been thinking what it would have been like to bring Sara here, to show her this beautiful place. He realized suddenly that he had been sitting at the table for a long time. He could hardly refuse. A woman and two men were standing behind the waiter, waiting for his reply.

"No, of course not. I won't be long. I've just ordered my coffee." He pulled his chair over to make more room. The strangers thanked him as they sat down. The tall man offered his hand politely.

"My name is David Anderson." Shahnawaz shook it and nodded his head in acknowledgment.

"Shahnawaz Khan."

The waiter brought the wine list, and the newcomers studied it intently. When the coffee arrived, Shahnawaz took a sip immediately, burning his throat. He wanted to leave as soon as possible.

David smiled.

"Please don't hurry; we appreciate you letting us sit with you. We weren't really up for waiting in the rain."

Shahnawaz tried to smile back.

"Not a problem," he said stiffly.

"These are my friends – Peter Jenkins, Claire Harris."

Peter and Claire shook hands too.

"This is the first decent place I've been to in a while," said Peter. "Just got back to the States yesterday. Three months leave. I've been stationed in Afghanistan."

Shahnawaz frowned and drew in his breath as if someone had shoved him.

Peter looked at him curiously.

"Are you okay?"

"My apologies," said Shahnawaz. "It is nothing."

The waiter arrived with the menu and the men began discussing what to order. Claire chose the first thing she saw, then did her best to read Shahnawaz's chiseled features. Who was this dark, sad stranger?

"Are you from Afghanistan?" she asked, unable to contain herself.

"Yes, yes," he answered. "I am." Gulping the rest of his coffee, he signaled the waiter. There was an awkward silence while he paid his bill, got up, and reached for his coat on a hook behind him. He left the restaurant without a word.

The friends exchanged glances as they watched him stride down the wet sidewalk.

"Weird guy," muttered Peter under his breath.

"Deeply strange," agreed David.

"He went pale when I mentioned Afghanistan," said Peter. "Like he'd seen a ghost."

Claire was more sympathetic.

"Maybe what you said about Afghanistan brought back painful memories."

"Maybe," said Peter.

The talk turned quickly to other things.

"Will you be here over Christmas?" asked David, smiling.

"Yes, thank God. I dread going back. It's a wretched place."

"It's your fault," said David, laughing. "No one forced you to join the army."

"You're right," said Peter quietly.

"You were so smart," said David, turning serious himself. "You could have gotten into Yale, or Harvard maybe. Why West Point?"

"I'm not sure. It seemed glamorous somehow. The discipline appealed to me."

"Glamour counted for a lot back in high school," added Claire. "And you were such a hard worker."

"But high school was only the beginning for my parents. They're sweet people, but I always felt they wanted more. They saw me as a doctor maybe, or a research scientist. Definitely an advanced degree. All I could think about was all those academics – studying on and on forever. I wanted something my own. I wanted something to happen."

The waiter brought their food.

* * *

The rain had turned to a thin drizzle, and Shahnawaz walked quickly through the icy night.

His evening was ruined. The strangers had invaded his privacy, shattered the fragile fantasy of Sara beside him, safe in this great city. Of her laughter and love. Of his daughter. He tried to imagine his baby as an eight-year-old, and saw nothing at all.

Here he was, an envied success story, a powerful businessman living in an elegant Manhattan neighborhood on a high floor, with expanses of glass overlooking the river. He owned several companies; had properties in prime locations. He drove a sleek black BMW. Yet all this was a distraction, not a source of happiness. Friends had done their best to involve him in the life of the city. But he had no desire for stylish women, fashionable restaurants or wild nights. He remained aloof and alone. No one took pride in his wealth and achievements. No one cared how much money he brought in this week, or what car he would choose to replace last year's model.

In Afghanistan, there had been nothing like this. But there had been happiness. His family had been well off, his father respected. His parents had doted on him; Raby worshipped him. Most of all, Sara adored him. The love of his life. Their two years together seemed like yesterday – and a lifetime ago.

Winning Sara had not been easy. She was the only daughter of a tribal lord, while he belonged to a middle class family. After four years of diplomatic courtship, of politeness and persistence, her father had finally consented to their marriage. The Air Force had seemed ideal for him, a sure rising trajectory. Until the attack that went awry. Where doing his duty had changed everything.

He went to bed as soon as he got home and lay in the dark, his eyes closed. He was bothered by his reaction in the restaurant. The stranger had only mentioned Afghanistan. He knew his abrupt departure had seemed rude.

Two hours later, sleep was still miles away. He switched on the light, for a moment blinded by the brightness. But he rubbed his eyes and picked up a book. After two or three pages, he realized that he had no idea what he had been reading. He slammed it shut and closed his eyes as hard as he could. He wanted to cry out, but there was no one to hear him. He opened the book again. This time, the story calmed him, and after fifteen or twenty minutes, he could feel his eyes getting heavy. But demon thoughts followed him into sleep.

In one dream, Natasha was learning to walk on her little fat feet, so happy with her achievement that she did not want to stop. She tottered on her wobbly legs from one piece of furniture to another, crowing at her success each time she reached a new handhold, then looking around for approval. Shahnawaz clapped his hands, made his mouth into a big silly O of delight and grinned, scooping her up in his arms, kissing her cheeks and holding her over his head while they laughed together, sharing her triumph.

Then he threw her up in the air, and she shattered into a million pieces.

* * *

In his waking moments, Shahnawaz was often irritable or distant. The memories sometimes made it difficult for him to breathe, even after all these years. He could feel his hands trembling. He had consulted doctors to find out why his body acted this way. Maybe, he thought, I have a disease.

Specialists examined him, ordered tests. The results were clear. He was perfectly healthy. They prescribed anti-anxiety drugs to ease his mind. He never bought the medicine. In truth, he did not want to dull the memories. They were all he had left – his only joy; his greatest pain; his punishment for being alive, for sleeping beneath smooth Pratesi sheets while his family lay under the heavy black earth of the grave.

* * *

The sun was up. The clock read 10 am. It was unheard of for him to rise so late. But this morning, he got ready for the office slowly. For years, he had driven himself to achieve. At work he had an outlet for anger and frustration, cramming his mind with plans and charts and strategy and figures, pushing his sorrows into a dark corner. Thus, he had built an empire. He gave many thousands of dollars to charity, and this brought him some solace. Still, the sorrows refused to crouch silently in the shadows. The void remained. He felt sadder than ever.

Chapter Two

When dinner was over, Peter and his friends parted ways. The stranger's odd behavior had ruined the mood of celebration.

Peter was eager to spend more time with Claire. He had missed her overseas. But today, he needed to go home and give his mind a rest. In Afghanistan, close encounters with misery and death had changed the way he approached things on the most basic level. He thought about life differently. He questioned his capacity for joy and laughter.

Peter Jenkins had grown up in a wealthy upper middle class New York family with one older sister. His father was a financial advisor on Wall Street; his mother, a dedicated teacher in a neighborhood high school. His parents loved each other, and their children. They still lived on Manhattan's Upper East Side, in a four story brownstone with a small garden.

David, Peter and Claire had gone to Bronx Science together, one of four top New York public high schools. There, Peter and Claire were inseparable. Afterwards, Claire stayed in the city to attend New York University; Peter went upstate to the prestigious military academy at West Point and majored in electrical engineering. When he visited New York, he and Claire spent the time together. He graduated near the top of his class. When he was posted to Afghanistan, there was talk of marriage. But they postponed their engagement until his return.

The American approach in Afghanistan was shifting away from fighting the terrorists directly to using troops to bolster the war-torn country and prepare it to function on its own. Many soldiers arrived with lofty ideas about helping people they saw as illiterate and backward. They considered themselves potential saviors, building schools and hospitals; training soldiers; helping to liberate women they saw as "enslaved" by custom, religion, and family. But they brought little understanding of the strength and meaning of Afghan tradition. Reality proved very different from what they had been told. Often, they were not welcomed at all.

Before his deployment, Peter never thought about his life of comfort and security. In Afghanistan, he was surprised by how much he missed it. He didn't take anything for granted any more. He was prepared to defend the country he loved. But in Afghanistan, his duty no longer seemed clear. How could this poor third world country, thousands of miles away, threaten America? The idea was laughable. And though every proud Afghan carried a rifle, it was crude or refurbished – no match for modern American weapons. Still, Afghans were willing to die to preserve their independence, and American personnel were still being maimed, even killed, almost every month.

Peter had been serving for nearly a year before this desperately needed break. He had witnessed poverty and cruelty, often inflicted by ignorant American troops. He had seen men die too – on both sides. Now, the thought of having to return to Afghanistan seemed almost unbearable.

* * *

The morning after their dinner together, Claire got a call from David.

"I was thinking of giving a party for Peter this Saturday," he told her. "But I need your help."

"That's a great idea; he does seem down. Maybe a party will cheer him up."

"I want to invite his friends. You know them better than I do. You could ask him who he wants there. Can you do that?"

"Of course." They went over the details together. Saturday was only three days away.

Claire asked Peter to meet her near her office for lunch. She was already running late. At dinner, she'd begun to feel that his experiences in Afghanistan were affecting him. He seemed more solemn and guarded than before – less spontaneous and full of fun. There was a darkness in him that she didn't recognize or understand.

* * *

Peter had awoken, as he often did, with Afghanistan weighing on his mind. His sleep had been fitful, broken by thoughts and images he could not suppress. It was hard to feel at home in this cozy top floor room, still decorated for a privileged New York teenager. He stared at the Green Day poster at the foot of his bed and thought about the war.

It was clear to Peter that he and his fellow soldiers were grappling with intractable problems, hampered by security restrictions and the obstinate pride of the Afghan people.

How were they supposed to build a new Afghanistan for a population actively hostile to those who intended to help them? What he had seen in Afghanistan raised a million questions. Why was he there? What had the Afghan people done to deserve such punishment? Why were American soldiers being killed and injured? Why? Why?

Most of all, he thought about his best friend, Luke Montgomery. They had shared a room at West Point. Then, Luke's Humvee had tripped an I.E.D. – a homemade roadside bomb – and both his legs were blown away. He was flown to Germany for treatment. Now, he was back in America.

That terrible day, Peter was supposed to take the lead on patrol. But he was dog tired, with a strep throat and high fever and asked Luke to go instead. Since then, he found himself racked with guilt that dogged him day and night. That bomb, he felt, had been meant for him. Instead, it had maimed Luke forever.

"What will I do without my legs?" Luke asked Peter. "I can't live like this. Jesus! Why didn't I die?" The words echoed again and again in Peter's mind. Luke called his injury "worse than death." Peter understood.

Luke's proud parents had believed that America was sending these handsome, brave young men on a mission of mercy. They expected their son back full of smiles, with stories of gratitude from the Afghan people. He had a job waiting for him on his return, and a pretty, eager girlfriend. But Afghanistan destroyed those dreams. The job was filled by someone available, and, the girl, unable to handle Luke's pain and anger, left to find someone new. To Peter, the damage to Luke's body were equaled by the maiming of his heart and soul.

How would Luke ever recover? And what could Peter say?

Thank you for taking the hit for me. For getting your legs blown away, instead of mine?

After the I.E.D., nothing was the same for Peter either. His nights were restless, he angered easily, he couldn't concentrate. Luke had lost his legs; Peter had lost his compass.

* * *

His mother's voice, calling up the stairs, broke into his anguished thoughts.

"Peter, what would you like for breakfast?"

"Oh, the usual, Mom," he called back from the landing. "Whatever."

"Come on, Petey. There must be something that sounds good to you." She was worried about the changes she sensed in her son. She wanted to make him eggs and bacon, pancakes, waffles – to find something that might help him feel better.

Peter looked down and managed a smile. It was not her fault that he was miserable. "Waffles," he said. "Waffles with syrup, Mom. Thanks."

* * *

After breakfast, Peter stood in the shower thinking about Luke. The phone rang, and he grabbed a towel, drying his hair while he talked. It was Claire.

"I've called you a bunch of times," she said, "but it keeps going to voicemail."

"Claire. It's so good to hear you." He really meant it. "How are you?"

"I'm fine. But I need to talk to you. How about meeting me for lunch?"

"Is that a request or an order?" Her energy made him smile.

"A request, of course! Please say yes – I have to ask you something."

"Yes, ma'am. Thank you, ma'am," he said, laughing. Her voice definitely made things better. "See you in forty five."

* * *

It was more like an hour. Claire was already at a table.

"Hi, honey," he said. He gave her a kiss on the cheek and slid into the booth facing her.

"I ordered a club sandwich for me and some coffee for you," said Claire. "Do you want a sandwich too?"

"No thanks, I just ate. So why did you drag me out of bed?"

"You were in bed at noon?" She felt a twinge of worry.

"Yes, I was, ma'am. A soldier has to make the most of his holiday." He paused a moment. "Well, not quite. Actually, I was in the shower." He remembered Luke, and his smile faded.

"So what's up, Claire? What's so important?"

Claire pushed her concerns away and gave him a big smile.

"Don't worry. It's something good. David wants to throw you a party, and he asked me to find out who you want him to invite. Anyone you'd like." Peter didn't return the smile.

"He wants to throw me a party?"

"Don't you like the idea?" His clear blue eyes were suddenly opaque. Claire could sense the beginnings of a frown.

"No, no. It's a great idea," he said without conviction. "I really appreciate how everyone is trying to welcome me home. But remember, I'm going back right after Christmas. I think about it all the time. I've seen a lot of bad things happen lately. I'm not in the mood for parties."

"I know it must be bad there. But try to let it go for now.

Enjoy yourself while you're here. It'll do you good, believe me.'

He stirred his coffee, staring down at the swirling brown liquid as if he were studying it.

"You don't know what it's like, Claire. When you're over there, you can't imagine living here. Back here, everyone is just living their lives as usual, but to me, it feels totally unreal now. I'm not a part of it. It's as if I'm looking in. We kill people, you know. And we get killed too. We're in danger at every step. It's not a computer game."

"Wow," said Claire. What he was saying was no surprise. She had read about feelings like this. But it was different to hear him say it. "It sounds to me like you really need this party, Peter. You need to be around old friends and see how much you mean to them. They care about you, Peter. We all do. Let yourself feel it. Please. I know you can." Her voice was filled with emotion.

They were both silent for a moment. He looked up at her and shrugged his shoulders. "You're probably right," he said, and managed a smile.

Who knows, he thought. *Maybe a party will help.* Besides, he felt grateful that Claire and David for making an effort to cheer him up. For their sake, he decided, he would do his best to show some enthusiasm.

"So it's okay?" Claire asked hopefully.

"Sure. Let's have a party."

"That's great," she said. Her smile was a grin now. She produced a folded piece of paper from the bottom of her bag.

"I had a few ideas," she said, smoothing the creases and crinkling her nose at him, a habit he had always found adorable. "Just a few names. See what you think." She handed him a long list. He glanced at it.

"It's fine, Claire. All fine. Invite who you want. I have no beef with anyone here." He gave an ironic smile. "I'm a good guy, remember? I like people; people like me. No Afghans on the list – they're the only ones who hate me."

"Don't be so melodramatic," said Claire, and gave his hand a squeeze. For the next few minutes, they went over the list together.

"Did I miss anyone?" Claire asked.

"Not really. But there is someone else – someone I want you to meet. A buddy who saved my life. In fact, I'm planning on seeing him later today. Maybe you'd like to come with me?"

"Of course! Who? Why don't we invite him to the party?"

"No go. He's in the Veterans' hospital on East 23rd Street."

"Oh, I'm sorry," said Claire. She wasn't sure what she should say.

"When do you get off work?"

"I can leave at five if you need me to." She wanted to make it clear that she was there for him.

"What if I pick you up at five fifteen?"

"Sure. Perfect." She squeezed his hand again. "So what's your friend's name?"

"Luke."

"Luke," she repeated. "Luke. Great. I'll buy him some flowers."

She finished her sandwich. Peter hardly touched his coffee.

Chapter Three

A night of tossing and turning and bad dreams had not improved Shahnawaz's mood. At the restaurant, all he had wanted was to cherish the memories of his wife and daughter, to hold them close in his mind – what they were, and what they could have been. His baby as a lovely little girl, almost grown; his beloved Sara, still at his side. But the unpleasantness at dinner had ruined everything. Bad enough that the three strangers had barged in and shattered his private fantasy; when they started talking about Afghanistan, his sadness was swept away by anger. America had brought untold misery to his people – he felt personally invaded too. The thought was not rational. Still, it was just too much.

In Afghanistan, thirty years of war had taken their toll. Educated Afghans, like Shahnawaz's family, lived primarily in the cities. The modest dress women were required to wear in public did not hamper their ability to learn. But most of his countrymen remained in remote villages where food was cooked on open fires, and clean water and electricity were unheard of luxuries. The frail died, but the strong became stronger, able to walk for miles, endure extreme heat or cold. Afghans were brave fighters, totally committed to their venerable tradition of self-government, passionately independent, and passionately loyal to their tribes and their families. They deserved respect, not patronizing or coercion.

It was getting light when Shahnawaz finally slept. At 10:30, he awoke feeling drained and lethargic. He dealt with crucial emails on his laptop, then lay in bed for another hour. It was afternoon before he left for work. *By the time I get there, most of the staff will be at lunch*, he thought, and delayed even longer.

Shahnawaz's office was in the financial district at the southern tip of Manhattan, not far from where the twin towers of the World Trade Center had once reached proudly for the sky. Business was thriving, but the richer he became, the lonelier he felt. He reached his office about one thirty. He handed his keys to the parking attendant, and the glossy BMW disappeared into the darkness of the garage. Still, he resisted going up to his office, persuading himself that a stroll might clear his mind.

The street was full of people returning to work after lunch. He walked aimlessly, mechanically, absorbed in his thoughts. The woman he bumped into seemed to come from nowhere. He reached out without thinking and grabbed her arm to steady her.

"I am so very sorry," he said. "Are you alright?" He bent over to pick up her bag from the sidewalk.

"Don't worry, I'm fine," she said, rearranging the strap on her shoulder. "Really."

The voice was oddly familiar. For the first time, he looked at her face. It was the young American woman from the night before.

"It's you," he said. "Didn't we meet last night? At the restaurant?"

"Yes, me." She grinned. "Were you expecting someone else?" She laughed.

"Claire? Or am I mistaken?"

"That's it. And you are Shahnawaz, right?"

"I'm impressed that you remembered. Do you work around here?"

"Over there," she replied, pointing to the gleaming tower behind him. "I'm with Dunbar Patton, in Document Production."

"How extraordinary! My office is in the same building. We're on the 23rd floor." He reached into his pocket and handed her an engraved business card. "If things don't work out with your current firm, come up and talk to me. Maybe I could find you something more interesting."

"Thank you so much," she said, surprised. She smiled broadly. "I'd give you a card too, but I don't have one with me," she continued. "But give me one of your cards, and I'll write my name and number on the back of it, just in case." She didn't really know why she had said this. "That is, if you want me to," she added awkwardly, and laughed. He found her delightful.

"I am so glad I ran into you," said Shahnawaz.

"You are?" she said, tilting her head and raising one eyebrow. "I thought you were sorry…" He was taken aback for a moment, and she watched him.

"I am. Truly," he continued, understanding the joke and smiling too. Then they both laughed together.

"But seriously," he continued, "I must apologize to you and your friends for my behavior last night. Please convey my apologies to everyone." His voice was very deep.

"No need to apologize. It was something we said, wasn't it? You were upset when we mentioned Afghanistan."

"Yes," he replied, surprised to find himself sharing his feelings with this stranger. "I am Afghan, you see," he added, unnecessarily. "The war has deeply affected us all."

"I saw that in your face," she said, full of sympathy. "I am so sorry."

"It is not your fault, surely," he continued. "No hard feelings?"

"None at all," said Claire, smiling again. Then she glanced at her watch and her face fell. "Oh dear, I'm late. I must get back to the office." They walked into the building together, then parted for separate banks of elevators.

* * *

Claire was ten minutes late when the elevator door opened. She hurried into the office, hoping to stay under the radar. But her supervisor Cathy Hardwick walked into the reception area as she entered. The woman always had a smile on her face, but in fact, she was always angry. She seemed to draw energy from finding fault, and she had no interest in excuses.

"Do you know what time it is?" said Cathy, clenching her teeth in a dreadful smile.

"I'm a little late. I know," replied Claire. "I'm so sorry."

"Ten minutes. You call that little?" Cathy's voice was flat, deadly calm.

"I am so sorry," Claire repeated.

"If this type of irresponsible behavior continues, you'll be looking for another job."

"It won't happen again. I'm very sorry."

"Well then, stop apologizing and get to work."

Claire bit her tongue to keep herself from saying "I'm sorry" again and walked to her desk frowning. She felt humiliated, as if Cathy had slapped her like a naughty child. She wanted to walk out that very moment, but she needed the job. She sat down, took a couple of deep breaths to calm herself, and turned her mind to her encounter with the gracious Afghan stranger.

* * *

Running into Claire had left Shahnawaz feeling inexplicably cheerful. He thought of her as he strode into his office, and she was still in his mind as his assistant went over his messages. Soon, he was fully absorbed in his work. When he looked at his watch again, the office had emptied out. It was already almost seven.

Soon, he thought, I'll be back in my empty apartment. Alone. Oddly, the idea was no longer disheartening. Nothing had changed, but he felt better than he had for a long time.

* * *

When the minute hand of the large superfluous wall clock registered 5 pm, Claire sighed with relief. She had been watching it for some time. Her mood rose with the thought of Peter waiting for her in the coffee shop. She was excited to meet the man who had saved his life. What kind of flowers, she thought, might cheer a wounded soldier? She got up and lifted her bag from the back of her chair.

Over her shoulder, she sensed her supervisor watching, like some predatory bird. "When you're ready to leave, I see, you manage to keep your eye on the time," said Cathy, her voice heavy with sarcasm. "Don't be late now…"

Claire ignored the remark. She had no desire to confront this obnoxious woman.

"Good night, Cathy," she said, her tone neutral. "See you tomorrow."

At the flower shop in the lobby, she bought a bunch of bright sunflowers. They seemed positive and masculine.

Peter had not yet arrived at the coffee shop, so she sat down and ordered a cappuccino. Waiting, she found herself thinking of Shahnawaz and the sadness she had seen in his eyes. For some reason, it worried her. She wanted to know exactly what had hurt him so badly. Those eyes were so dark they were almost black, with long, heavy lashes – compelling, beautiful, set off by a defined mouth and high chiseled cheekbones. He was, she realized suddenly, a very handsome man. She was glad that she knew how to reach him now. She could call him up whenever she wanted to, though she couldn't imagine why she would. She was wondering what she could say if she did, when she felt a hand on her shoulder.

She jumped.

"I didn't know I was that scary." Peter was standing behind her, grinning.

"I didn't see you." She grinned back. "But you are pretty scary, come to think of it. Want some coffee?"

"No time. Visiting hours are over at seven thirty."

There was no getting a cab at this time of day. They walked to the subway, holding hands. People swirled around them.

* * *

The hospital was busy too, full of after-work visitors coming to see their loved ones. The halls were an unappealing beige, relieved by an occasional meaningless abstract print. They passed a gift shop full of pre-arranged flowers, boxes of candy and Mylar balloons.

To Peter's enormous relief, Luke seemed happy to have visitors. His attitude had changed hugely since Peter had last seen him. Somehow, he seemed to have made his peace with the trauma that had disrupted his life. He greeted Claire and the sunflowers with enthusiasm. She busied herself finding something to put them in.

"You seem a lot better, Luke," said Peter. "What's up?"

"I am better, man. At the beginning, those idiot doctors didn't think I would make it. I didn't think so myself. But I met some amazing guys who got through similar stuff, and I worked with a great counselor. And against all odds, here I am – back home and out of the woods."

In spite of his optimistic words, Claire was shocked to see how badly he was wounded. An ugly scar across one cheek had taken off the end of his eyebrow, barely missing his eye. His forearm was still thickly bandaged. The covers flattened below his knees, where there was nothing at all.

"War is brutal," she said, almost to herself. "It's so hard to imagine; it must be terrible over there." She stopped. "I'm sorry, Luke. I have no business talking like that."

"Nothing to be sorry about," he replied. "That's the way it is. Got to man up. What you see is what you get."

Peter concentrated on changing the subject.

"How long are they keeping you here?" he asked.

"I get sprung from the hospital soon, but they want me to stay in New York for rehab. I need to start training for my prosthetics right away. What they can do these days is incredible, man. I'm really lucky I still have my knees. If you don't, the legs are much harder to fit. Knees make it much easier to move them too."

"So what's next, Luke?" Peter continued. "Are you going to stay in the service?"

"I don't know. Prosthetics are so good these days that some guys even go back into the field – but I've had it with combat. I'm not up for getting more parts blown off, that's for sure."

"I'm sure you'll figure it out," chimed in Claire, doing her best to sound positive.

"Maybe," he said politely.

Then he turned to Peter, and his voice took on a more urgent tone. "You know, Pete, I joined up to serve my country – not to go after a bunch of third world guys who don't even threaten us. Most of them want us out of there."

"I get it, Luke. Believe me. You're preaching to the choir."

"So what about you?"

"I'm here for Christmas, thank God. Then back there by January."

"I bet they'll end this damn war soon – they've got to."

"I hope so," said Claire.

Luke smiled at her. "He's tough," he said. "And smart. He'll be fine. And home in one piece before you know it."

"You're right, I'm sure," said Claire, giving Peter's arm a squeeze. But she didn't feel sure at all.

A nurse came in and looked pointedly at her watch. "He needs his rest, you know," she said kindly. Visiting hours were over.

* * *

Winter darkness cloaked the city as Claire and Peter started uptown. They walked in silence for a while, close to each other, but not touching, absorbed in their own thoughts.

In spite of Luke's positive attitude, the visit to the hospital left Claire shaken by the ugly realities of war. She had seen war movies. Films these days didn't sugarcoat modern conflict – they stressed boredom, frustration and ambivalence – not glory. Still, it was different to actually meet someone whose life had been completely derailed.

She found herself thinking of how casualties reverberated through families; of spouses leaving memorial services with nothing but a folded American flag and a medal; of kids who never really understood where Dad had gone. To be injured like Luke meant mangled lives, devastated dreams. And what about the battered psyches? Veterans full of secret fears and anger, not themselves anymore? And there were those who opted for suicide.

It didn't matter that Luke seemed reconciled to his condition – that he was actually looking forward to his artificial limbs. If he'd never gone, he would be walking on his own two legs and honeymooning with his girlfriend.

"Peter," she said, her voice full of resolve. "When you come home again, your service obligation will be over. I want you to resign your commission."

"What? You're not serious."

"I'm very serious."

"It's not that easy, Claire."

"You could end up like Luke."

"You think I don't know that? I have no illusions. But I do have obligations. People are counting on me. What do I tell them? 'Hey, guys, I've had enough. I'm going home.'" Peter gave a laugh, but there was nothing joyful in the sound.

"This is the time to think about it, Peter. While you are home."

"No way, Claire. My men are still out there. I can't just stay here and get married and lead my life. Don't ask me to do that."

Claire was quiet for a moment. Neither of them was ready for this conversation. She had hadn't even had a chance to get to know this new, different Peter since he had returned. She changed the subject.

"Okay, Peter. Let's think about good things. Tonight, for example. Are you tired? Do you want to go home and take it easy?"

"No, no. That's the last thing I want. Tonight is for you. How about dinner? And a club later. When did you last go dancing?"

"A century ago. At least. Yes, please. Take me dancing." She felt hugely relieved. It was exactly what she wanted. And, she thought, it's important for him to enjoy himself here, in the moment.

"At your command, my love."

"Perfect," Claire said. That sounded like the old Peter. "Absolutely perfect."

"There's a cab," said Peter, spotting a lighted taxi with a New Yorker's seasoned eye. "I'll drop you off and give you an hour to make yourself beautiful. Then, I will appear at your door – your gallant prince, ready to sweep you away."

As they got into the cab, her earlier chance meeting came to mind.

"Guess who I bumped into this afternoon?"

"Who?" asked Peter.

"Shahnawaz," she told him, delighted, as if she had run into an old friend.

"Who?"

It seemed incredible that Peter wouldn't remember him. "You know, Shahnawaz. The man who let us sit at his table last night. Isn't that an amazing coincidence?"

"Oh yeah," said Peter, frowning. "You mean the guy who was so rude to us? How do you know his name?"

"He introduced himself. Don't you remember?" Peter looked irritated. She couldn't imagine why.

"Yes, I do remember. Then he got up and stalked out like some kind of maniac. Remember that?"

"Well, he apologized to me for his behavior. And he asked me to apologize to you and David too."

"That was nice of him," said Peter, not at all mollified. "So I guess you two had a nice long talk. Did you?"

"Peter, what is wrong with you? Why are you angry with that poor man?"

"Never mind, it's nothing," he said. He took a deep breath and tried to show some interest. "So how did you meet him?"

"I was late for work when I left you – all I could think about was getting back before Cathy noticed the time. And I just wasn't paying attention. I literally bumped into him. It was so weird. I looked up, and there he was."

* * *

Claire felt excited when she reached her apartment. There was a lot to do. She wanted to be perfect for Peter.

She took a shower and spent half an hour blowing, drying her hair. The gleaming result was worth the effort. She chose a little black dress she knew she looked good in. It came up high in the front, with a sparkly band around her throat. But when she turned around, it had no back at all. Her shoes had delicate straps around the ankles too, with bows on them. The heels were thin and high, but not too high for dancing.

She put a dark line along her eyelashes, and soft, smoky eye shadow. She was pleased when she looked at her image in the mirror. She knew that Peter would be pleased too. The bell rang at twenty minutes to nine.

She opened the door. Peter was wearing a black suit and a white shirt that set off his tan, a golden legacy of the harsh Afghan sun. He looked strong and masculine and handsome, the very best of America.

"Hello!" She said, kissing him lightly. "You are ten minutes late." She smiled. "Lucky I'm not Cathy," she added. "I might just slam the door on you."

"Then I'm glad you're Claire," he replied, smiling, and stepping back to look at her. His expression changed.

"What's the matter?" Claire asked. "You look so serious."

"You know, baby, you are beautiful. Really beautiful."

He pulled her inside and shut the door. He put his arms around her waist, and leaned back to look into her eyes. "I am very, very lucky to have you, my darling. Thanks for looking so pretty for me."

Then he bent her over and kissed her passionately. She returned the kiss, then drew back, smiling.

"Very flattering," she said, raising one eyebrow. "But I thought you asked me out to dinner. That doesn't seem to be the direction we're going in…"

"Oh, so you want dinner," said Peter, smiling again. "Greedy girl."

"Yes, I do. I've been waiting to have dinner alone with you for a long, long time."

* * *

The evening was wonderful – surprising and original cocktails, followed by excellent wine and delicious food. They ended up at a club full of young beautiful people, with candlelit nooks and crannies that offered privacy too. People were dancing and laughing. A dark-eyed man gazed at Claire from the bar. When the music segued to a new song, he came towards her.

"Would you honor me with this dance, Madame?" He asked gallantly, holding out his arm.

"No, she would not," said Peter firmly, taking Claire's arm himself. "She's with me."

"I asked her, not you," said the man, clearly irritated. "She can answer."

"Thank you so much," said Claire quickly. "I think I'll sit this one out." She could feel Peter's muscles tense beneath his jacket.

The man bowed his head, glared at Peter and walked away. She felt hugely relieved and determined to defuse the moment.

"That wasn't very nice, Peter," said Claire playfully, doing her best to keep things light. "He was great looking. I might have enjoyed dancing with him."

"Sorry, Claire," he replied, looking at her seriously. "But you need to concentrate on me until I go back to Afghanistan. I intend to be with you every possible moment."

"After that," he added, "you are on your own. I may come back… or I may not. If I don't, you can play around with other guys as much as you please."

"Don't be such a pessimist," said Claire firmly. "I don't play around. You know that. And you will come back. We will probably be married before you know it."

Then she was quiet for a moment, and her face darkened. She felt acutely aware of the people swirling around them, laughing and talking – their minds a million miles from the rugged hills of Afghanistan, the miseries of the Afghan people or the American soldiers serving there. She thought of Luke in his hospital bed. She thought of the sadness in Shahnawaz's eyes. Peter saw the emotions shadowing her face.

"Forget it, Claire. Don't listen to my craziness, please. I brought you here for a good time."

It occurred to her that Peter assumed that she had been worrying about him. But she lifted her face to him and smiled. "Okay," she said. "Your call. Let's have fun," and she pulled him onto the dance floor again. It was the last time they mentioned the subject.

It was 2 am when Claire looked at her watch.

"Oh dear," she said, exasperated. "We have to get out of here – I'll never make it to the office tomorrow."

"Of course, hon, I'll get you home. Let's go."

* * *

The wind was a shock as they stepped into the night. A lone bus was pulling out from the curb, but there was almost no traffic. Mercifully, a few blocks away, a yellow cab with a light on the roof was coming towards them – an empty cab. Peter opened the door for her, helped tuck in her coat, then folded his long legs and slid in beside her. He gave the cabbie the address, turned to her, and put his hand on her knee. He ran his fingers softly through her long curls. Her hair was thick and smooth and cool. He kissed her slowly, just a little. If he himself let go, he would not be able to leave her.

Claire knew instinctively what he was feeling. She felt the same way herself. When they pulled up at her apartment building, he got out of the cab and came around to open the door for her. She stood at the edge of the sidewalk, standing apart from him, holding his hands. He gave a small sad smile.

"So it goes," he said, and kissed her gently, almost like a brother. "Sleep well, baby." She let go of his hands and touched his cheek.

"Thank you, Peter. It was wonderful."

As the cab drew away, he pressed his palm against the window. She felt a wave of sadness and reached out her hand for a moment, as if to keep him from slipping away from her. When she turned, the doorman had already opened the door, and she stepped through into the light.

Chapter Four

CB

Shahnawaz found himself calmer after running into Claire. That night, he fell asleep without a pill and woke up refreshed. The sensation was unfamiliar. *Am I feeling happy?* he asked himself. *Is that possible?*

For the first time in years, the miseries he and his country had endured were not his first conscious thoughts. The sadness was still there, of course, but somehow, he sensed a new acceptance of his losses – and even a glimmer of hope for the future. *This won't last*, he thought. Still, he wanted to cherish the feeling.

He made himself a cup of tea and got ready for work. For some time, he had been coming in late – often, not before noon. But today, he was at his desk by nine thirty.

He felt energized, keenly interested in what was going on. Through the glass wall of his office, he noticed a number of empty desks and called his assistant Janet in and asked her to compile a list of late arrivals. Ten of his thirty employees were not even there yet. The ones who had arrived seemed disturbed to see him. There was a flurry of cell phone activity. News of his unusual behavior traveled fast.

Shahnawaz called his office manager into his office. "Steve," he said, "where is everybody? What the hell is going on?"

Steve sighed. He had nothing good to say. He had been late himself – a fact he did not mention.

"I am sorry, sir. But the truth is, since you have been coming in so late on a regular basis, people have taken advantage of your schedule. I've talked to them. There are, of course, excuses. But discipline should have been tighter, I know.

"In their defense," he continued, "I want you to know that people often stay late to finish their work. You have dedicated employees, sir. They depend on your leadership. Otherwise, I would have brought this up sooner."

By eleven, the work stations were full, and Shahnawaz called the entire staff into the conference room that adjoined his office.

They shuffled in, looking anxious, and when the chairs were filled, the rest lined up behind them in front of vast windows overlooking New York Harbor. He stood at the end of the rosewood table and looked from face to face. A number of them hardly met his gaze.

"When I arrived this morning," he said quietly, "I was surprised to see that only one third of my staff members were present. Is there some reason why so many of you were late?"

No one volunteered an explanation.

"Well?" he asked again. "I would really like to know."

His employees looked at each other. A few glanced out of the window as if seeking clarification in the clouds outside.

"I understand," he said, feeling his anger rising, "that you have been setting your own schedules. But you must understand too. It took a lot of work to build this business, and it has succeeded through dedication and discipline. This kind of behavior will destroy it." He paused for a moment, frowning, and looked around again.

"Look at me," he said. "Everyone." Slowly, eyes turned to his. "What should I do?" It was not a question. "I can't fire all of you, but you need to understand how serious this is. So this is how it's going to work. I am cutting salaries ten percent across the board for three months. Objections? Anyone? If so, tell me now. Right now. You can resign today. You'll get your full pay up to this moment."

Nobody spoke.

"Well, yes or no? Where do we stand? Do you care about this business? Do I have your support?" He paused. "If not, I do not want you here. Who is with me and who goes?"

No one broke the silence, but the room buzzed with invisible anxious energy. It was clear he had made a deep impression. Shahnawaz felt powerful; he was enjoying himself.

Then, slowly, people started talking, accepting his conditions. Jennifer Castillo, always level-headed and loyal, was the first to step forward. Even Paul Gregory, a brilliant but aggressive manager renowned for his arrogance, declared his commitment to the firm. Many employees shook Shahnawaz's hand and thanked him, acknowledging their errors. They told him they felt privileged to be working for him; they guaranteed their allegiance and vowed to arrive at the office on time. After a few minutes, things settled. Shahnawaz saw people looking at him, as if waiting for a signal.

"OK everyone," he said. "Let's get to work." He glanced down at the rich patterned grain of the conference table, and smiled to himself.

People filed back to their work stations, talking quietly, patting each other on the back. Soon, Shahnawaz was alone. He rubbed his eyes with his fingers.

There is no need to show such negative emotion, he thought. *One cannot compel loyalty. Anger is not the way.* Instantly, his thoughts returned to Afghanistan and the bitter past. He vividly remembered crossing the Pakistani border, the darkness of the night, the moment he had said goodbye to his country. At that moment, of course, he had fully expected to return.

* * *

The morning after Shahnawaz slipped out to visit his father's grave, Wahab Khan entered the brothers' room quietly and, for a few moments, stood watching, just inside the doorway. He had not been pleased when his guards had informed him that Shahnawaz had gone out during the night. But now, he embraced both young men.

"It is time," he said. "The truck is outside. You must sit in the back." He handed each of them a heavy black turban – the kind worn by the Taliban. "Do not let the driver stop for a second until you cross into Pakistan."

The time for words was over. Shahnawaz clasped Wahab Khan's hands in silence, but the old man saw the gratitude in his eyes.

The brothers tied on the turbans and climbed into the truck. The man at the wheel was tiny and shriveled. He looked too old to drive.

But at Wahad Khan's command, the truck jerked, then started moving, moving out of Shahnawaz's past, into an unknown future. They jolted over the rocky roads and Rubnawaz bent his head, praying for their father's soul.

They crossed the border before dawn, pressing on for many hours through the Khyber Pass and down onto the plain, past small villages, and the walled compounds of tribal lords, towards the provincial capital of Peshawar and into the crowded streets of the city itself. After only ten hours, their lives had changed entirely.

* * *

Shahnawaz's friend Jamshed had arranged for them to stay with Sabir Khan and his family. The enterprising Sabir had set up several shops in the area long ago. He offered the brothers honest work, and they accepted with gratitude. They settled into a routine, though life was neither pleasant nor easy.

Shahnawaz remained in contact with Jamshed Khan. But his friend was becoming increasingly gloomy; talks with the Tabani were not going as planned.

"After killing your family, the old man is drunk with power," Jamshed told him over the phone. "I fear he will not rest until he has shed your blood as well."

"To hell with him," said Shahnawaz. "I won't rest either until his family is deader than my own."

"More bad news, I'm afraid," Jamshed continued, ignoring the outburst. "I have not been able to get your leave extended. Tabani must have a mole here. He means to force you to return to Afghanistan."

"So be it." Shahnawaz said matter-of-factly. "I will lose my post."

"I will keep trying," said Jamshed. "Goodbye, my friend. And good luck."

* * *

Shahnawaz ceased his reverie and forced his mind back to the present. How far he had come over ten years. Afghanistan, Pakistan – they were his past. He had forged a business anyone could be proud of. He would not let it fail. He vowed to himself to change his work ethic. To be vigilant; to rededicate himself to the enterprise he had built and loved; to rise above self-pity and be a leader, once more worthy of his name and his heritage.

Then he took a deep breath and turned his back to the room, gazing out of the window at the harbor and the distant figure of Liberty raising her torch to enterprise, to hope, to the possibilities of America. *This morning's near fiasco was my fault*, he thought. *We are back on track, yes. But it cannot happen again.*

Chapter Five

CB

Claire was tired by the end of the day on Friday, glad to be back in her apartment on Manhattan's East Side, near the United Nations. It was a small space with a tiny bedroom, but she didn't mind. It was all hers.

She did some yoga stretches, took a shower, put on her favorite over-sized T shirt, and stretched out on the sofa. She closed her eyes for a moment, and Shahnawaz's handsome face immediately came to mind. She wished he was coming to the party, she realized. But she knew Peter wouldn't understand. She was not sure she understood herself.

Why would I invite someone I hardly know? she thought. It wasn't as if that first meeting had been fun. Then, their second encounter swam into her thoughts, eclipsing her negative feelings entirely.

She wanted very much to talk to Shahnawaz. Right now. Impulsively, she grabbed her bag, pulled out his card and her phone and entered his number.

"Hello." The sound of his deep, unmistakable voice, with its slight, intriguing accent froze her. She felt uncharacteristically shy.

Lord, she thought, *what was I thinking?*

"Hello?" he said again, sounding impatient.

Her number was on his screen now. Clearly, it was too late to hang up.

"Hello, Shahnawaz," she said at last. "It's me, Claire. Remember?"

"Claire? Yes, of course I remember you. How could I forget?"

"Actually, I'm not really sure why I called. I just found your card in my bag, and I wanted to say hello." It sounded feeble to her as she said it. But she had to say something – and it was, essentially, the truth.

"I'm so glad you did. I wanted to ring you myself. But I lacked the courage to do so." That was the truth too. "How are you?"

"Fine," said Claire, suddenly feeling very fine indeed.

"In fact," continued Shahnawaz, "I was thinking how much I would like to invite you to dinner. That is, if you'd allow me. But then, I wasn't sure it was appropriate."

"Oh no – I mean, yes, it's completely fine. Call me any time." *It must be hard,* she thought, *to be an Afghan in this country. It's only right* to *make him feel welcome.*

"I will call you," said Shahnawaz, sounding relieved. "What type of food do you prefer?"

"I don't really care," she said. "I love to eat. Chinese is great – Italian, Mexican."

"I will keep that in mind," he said, laughing. The laughter felt good.

"What about you?"

"I eat just about anything – but I still have a great fondness for Afghan cooking."

"Wonderful," said Claire. "I've never tasted Afghan food. What's it like?"

"Flatbread, of course. A good deal of lamb. And rice, with almonds and raisins, sometimes lemon and pistachios. The aroma is marvelous. And *firni* – a dessert like a creamy cloud full of cardamom and rosewater."

"Sounds delicious," said Claire, meaning it.

"You wouldn't by any chance be free tomorrow night, would you? I know an excellent Afghan restaurant on Second Avenue. Not fancy, but warm and friendly, and the food is authentic. It makes me feel at home."

"Oh no," said Claire. For a second, she had totally forgotten the party. "I'm sorry. Tomorrow we're throwing a party in honor of Peter – my friend who has to go back to Afghanistan." She felt oddly resentful about having to turn down the invitation, as if the party were intruding on potential time with Shahnawaz.

"Not to worry. Perhaps we can try it some other evening? Soon, I hope." He felt inordinately happy that Claire had rung him.

"Absolutely. Is next week good for you?"

"I am sure that I can find the time. I'll look at my schedule and give you a call. Is that ok?"

"Of course," she replied, relieved that he had not been put off by her refusal. "I wrote down my number for you, remember?" She paused. "And you have it on your phone now too – since I've called."

"Excellent," he laughed. "I have it twice now."

* * *

On Saturday, Claire focused all her energy on Peter's party. David's colleague Nelson had owed him a favor, and offered his Brooklyn penthouse for the evening. It was perfect – mostly a big, open, space, with a terrace overlooking over the East River. Nelson was heading to Gstaad for a week of skiing before Christmas. He was delighted that David could use it.

"Just leave the place clean," he said.

"I'll do my best," said David, with a grin.

Following Claire's list, David had sent e-vites to Peter's old friends – and added a few of his own. For David, the cost of the party was not an issue. But he was happy to divide the responsibilities with Claire, who took charge of the food and decorations.

Delighted to have something positive to do, she was determined to surround Peter with friends and love. People were coming at eight. Claire was very organized; by five, the food had been delivered. The flowers were done and the drinks set up. By five thirty, David was there to help too.

Claire had worn a black pencil skirt, but brought the rest of her party clothes with her. She left David dealing with the bartender while she went to get ready, luxuriating for fifteen minutes in Nelson's glass and marble shower. She did her makeup, then slipped on a red silk top scattered with sequins and red satin sandals with spike heels. After all, it was almost Christmas.

Just before eight, the bell rang. The room filled quickly. Soon, there were guests everywhere, laughing and drinking. It was David who noticed that Peter was missing. He looked around for Claire and found her absorbed in conversation.

"Hey, Claire," he said. "No Peter yet. Do you have his cell number?"

"Of course," she said, feeling immediately guilty for not noticing his absence.

"Well, call him and tell him that we're waiting for him. After all, this is supposed to be his party."

Peter answered on the second ring.

"It's me, Peter. Where are you? Everyone is here. Except you."

"I'm coming as fast as I can," said Peter, sounding tense. "There was an accident on the bridge, and we were stuck in a mess of traffic. But it's cleared up now. I'll be there in a few minutes."

"I'm so glad you're okay. I thought you might have forgotten us." Claire laughed, feeling relieved on many levels.

"Not a chance," said Peter. "You must think I've really lost it." There was a moment of silence.

"Well, hurry up," said Claire. "We need you." She closed her phone and turned to David.

"He's on his way," she said. "Traffic."

"I sure hope so," said David. "What an idiot. He should have called."

That's weird, thought Claire. *He must have left late. The old Peter would have called. Something's different.*

At nine, Peter walked in with an apologetic smile. People came rushing over to greet him. Claire hung back for a moment, her mind racing. *Why didn't I notice he was missing?* she thought. *What's the matter with me? I'm supposed to be in love with this man.*

Soon, Peter was laughing and talking, surrounded by friends, men thumping him on the back, women hugging him. He seemed to be drinking a lot, Claire noticed. But then again, so was David. She limited herself to a few glasses of wine – she never drank much at parties.

She danced with Peter – and with other men too. She noticed people watching her. It amused her, for she felt comfortable in her body, and she loved dancing. She was enjoying herself. It was fun to show off a little.

Her arms were swaying in the air and her eyes closed, when Peter came up behind her.

"Enough!" he said into her ear. He sounded angry. She stopped, frowning, and turned to him.

"I need to talk to you," he continued, grabbing her arm so hard it almost hurt. She thought of their evening in the nightclub, when the stranger had asked her to dance. He had been angry then too.

She pulled her arm away from him.

"I'm sorry, James," she said to the man she'd been dancing with. "But I need to talk to Peter now."

"No problem," he said, and backed off, eager not to be involved.

"What is going on, Peter?" she said quietly, "James must think you're crazy."

"I don't care what he thinks," said Peter. "I don't like it when you dance that way."

"Funny," she said. "You always liked it before."

"Don't be sarcastic," said Peter. "This is serious."

Suddenly, she felt embarrassed, acutely aware of the people around them. The glass doors to the terrace were only a few feet away. She took Peter's hand and pulled him outside, away from the crowd.

It was clear and very cold. The sky was full of stars; in the distance, the city glittered across the dark water. There was a large pot with a dead plant on the terrace beside them.

"Come on, Peter. You know I like dancing. What's this all about?"

"I really don't need you bringing attention to yourself like that. You belong to me."

He was leaning over her. His breath smelled like liquor.

"What are you talking about? What are you saying?"

"I'm supposed to just sit back and watch you throw yourself at other men?"

"This is insane, Peter. I'm not throwing myself at anyone. I'm just having a good time."

"Well, I'm not." His tone darkened. "I told you I didn't want a party, didn't I? Who are all these people anyway? They think they know me, but they don't."

"They're your friends."

"Sure. They're my friends, and you're my girl, and everything's great and everyone's happy. You live your fancy lives in this pretty city and spend fortunes on food and dance like there's no tomorrow. But you know nothing. Any of you." His voice was rising. "I can't take this anymore. I'm getting out of here."

He turned abruptly, slid the door open, and stepped back into the room, almost tripping over the metal door sill. He wove his way unsteadily around the crowd, and disappeared.

Claire stood for a moment, stunned, then realized that she was shivering all over. She stepped back into the warmth of the living room, sliding the door shut behind her, and made her way to the bedroom. A large pile of coats covered the bed. Peter's heavy leather jacket was gone.

Claire sat down on someone's scarf. She was shaking. She found her bag and tried Peter's phone. She dialed him three times, but there was no answer. In the living room, the party was in full swing.

She didn't understand what had happened. She and David had tried so hard to make Peter feel good – she couldn't believe that after all that, he had left his own party. And he had flown off the handle for no reason. After all this time, didn't he even trust her? At least he had gone quietly. No one seemed to have noticed.

Is this my fault? she wondered. *There must be something else going on. Why won't he tell me?* She crossed her arms over her chest and sat there for a minute, hugging herself.

This is still a good party, she thought. *Everyone's having a good time. I'm not going to spoil it just because Peter's being weird. I won't let him ruin it for his friends – or for me.*

She asked one of the servers to make her a cup of coffee, wrapped herself in her scarf, and stood out on the terrace drinking it. The wind from the river was sharp, but bracing. She didn't mind. After a few minutes, she went inside again. David danced up to her, grinning.

"Peter left," she said. "I'm not sure why. He'd had too much to drink, I think. And he was mad about something."

"The hell with him," said David amiably. "He'll be fine in the morning." The music rose, and he pulled her into the dancers.

Going on without Peter wasn't as hard as she had imagined. Part of her was relieved not to have to worry about him – he would be on his way home in a cab now, soon sleeping it off in his childhood bed. His mother would be there for him. *Everything will be all right*, she thought. *Poor Peter.*

She closed her eyes again and gave herself over to the music.

* * *

By one thirty, the last guests had gone. Only Claire and David remained. The catering people had already done most of the cleanup. David sat on the sofa looking dazed. Claire bustled around, fluffing pillows, straightening chairs, putting on the final touches.

She stepped back and surveyed her handiwork.

"Beeootiful," said David, slurring the word slightly. "Perfec'." He dropped the final t. "Wouldn't know a fly had been here. I'll drop you off. Got my car."

Claire gave him a skeptical look.

"I don't know, David. How many drinks have you had? Let's take a taxi."

"What? You want me to leave my car in Brooklyn? No way. Besides," he added, enunciating carefully. "I am an ex-cell-ent driver."

She raised an eyebrow.

"And it's the middle of the night," he added. "No one will be out driving anyway."

"I don't think it's a great idea. You can get your car tomorrow."

"I am taking my car tonight, Claire. Definitely. It'll be fine. Don't be chicken." He gave a loony grin.

"Okay," said Claire with a sigh. *I have to get home anyway,* she thought. *At least he'll have someone with him.*

* * *

David was right – traffic was scarce. The only people on the road, it seemed, were drunk drivers. One swerved into their lane, sound system blaring, and David leaned on the horn hard. The driver overcompensated and almost hit another car.

"What an asshole," said David, cheerfully. Claire crossed her arms tight.

The next one came up too fast behind them. David didn't even see him. There was a squeal of brakes, then a crunching sound, and the airbags exploded.

By some miracle, David managed to stop the car.

The rest was a nightmare, a swirl of sirens and blinking lights, policemen and paramedics. Both drivers tested positive for alcohol. The other driver would have to shoulder the blame for hitting David from behind. But insurance disputes would come later. First, everyone had to be checked for injuries.

Claire, who could walk on her own, persuaded the EMTs to take her in the same ambulance as David. As the doors closed, they heard the siren of a second ambulance carrying the driver who had hit them off into the night.

Chapter Six

CB

It was almost 4 am when the ambulance pulled up to the Emergency Entrance of Bellevue Hospital. Claire and David submitted to a battery of tests and were admitted for observation. Dawn was breaking before Claire managed a fitful sleep. She woke up to the sound of tinkling bells. It took her a minute to recognize her cell phone ringing – and to find it.

"Hello?" she said, uncertain for a moment where she was.

"Hello. Is that Claire?" The voice sounded familiar, but she couldn't quite place it.

"Yes." she said. "Yes it is."

"This is Shahnawaz speaking, Claire. You said that I could call, I believe? I wondered if you would be free for dinner this evening? I hope I am not disturbing you."

"Oh. Hello. Shahnawaz. Of course. I am so glad you called." She sat up, unconsciously smoothing her hair. "Actually, I'm in the hospital right now. I am not sure if they will discharge me today or not."

"That is terrible, Claire. What happened? Are you all right? Which hospital?"

"Bellevue, I think. On First Avenue. I'm fine. Really. But on the way back from the party last night, our car was hit by a drunk driver."

"We?"

"Oh, my friend David was driving me home. You know, you met him in the restaurant. The shorter man, with the brown hair."

"Yes, I remember him. And there was another friend with you also. The man who had returned from Afghanistan for his Christmas break." Shahnawaz remembered all three of them very clearly.

"You have a good memory," said Claire, managing a smile.

"Is your friend David all right?"

"I haven't seen him yet this morning. But he's okay, I think. They just wanted to make sure, so they kept us overnight."

"That is excellent news," said Shahnawaz. "I would very much like to come and see you now," he continued, surprising himself. He had not planned to say that at all. "I can be there in twenty minutes." For a moment, Claire didn't know what to say.

"That is," he added, "if you don't mind."

Claire laughed in spite of herself. Her head hurt.

"No, no, Shahnawaz. I need some time to get my head together. I don't even know when visiting hours are. It's still morning."

"I hate to correct you, Claire. And, of course, I will wait if you prefer. But it is almost three thirty in the afternoon."

"Really?" said Claire, astonished. "I can't believe I slept so long."

"Listen, Claire. I am coming."

"Wait," said Claire, "My last name is Harris." She realized

how little Shahnawaz knew about her – though, oddly, she felt she had known him for a very long time.

"I know. Claire Harris," said Shahnawaz, as if savoring her name. He gave a wonderful deep laugh. "You wrote it with your phone number. Do not go anywhere. I will be with you very soon."

Then he was gone.

Claire was fully awake now. She rang the button for the nurse and a few minutes later, a round brown face appeared in the doorway enhanced by elaborately braided hair and a radiant smile.

"You need me, honey?" she asked.

"Oh no," said Claire. "I'm okay right now. But I need to know about David Anderson. He came in the ambulance with me."

"He's just down the hall, in Room 608. His condition is stable. He has an itty bitty concussion and some whiplash, but he'll be 100 percent in a day or two." She sounded as if she were delivering wonderful news. "The doctor will probably keep him another night. But don't worry, honey, you are A-okay. When Dr. Gonzales does rounds later, he'll sign your discharge papers, and you'll be out of here."

"That," said Claire, "is good to hear." She smiled at the nurse and said a small silent prayer for David's health.

Then she dug in her purse for a mirror, a comb and some lip gloss. She wanted to look decent for Shahnawaz.

Again, her cell phone rang. *Maybe he forgot to tell me something*, she thought, and answered without looking at the number.

"Hello, Claire." It was Peter. "I acted badly last night. I want to apologize." Claire didn't say anything. She hadn't expected to hear Peter. She hadn't even thought of Peter at all.

"You know, all those people were just too much for me to handle." He paused. "And maybe I had too much to drink."

"You think so?" said Claire drily. She did her best to keep her thoughts straight. She wasn't sure what she felt about Peter right now.

"Listen, baby, I'm sorry. I said some things I shouldn't have. It just killed me to see you acting like that. Like nothing mattered to you."

"Like nothing mattered? The truth is, Peter, I don't understand what's going on with you. I was just having a good time. It's not like you never saw me dance before. You were so angry – but why? It was your party and everyone was happy to be with you." She felt at a loss for words.

"You know," she continued, "I really have a headache now. I hardly slept last night after the accident. Maybe we could talk later."

"Accident? What are you talking about?"

She sighed. But when she tried to explain what had happened, she could hear the anger in Peter's voice once more. He was angry at David for driving drunk, angry at her for going with him. He said that he was coming to the hospital now and would stay there until she was ready to go.

She didn't think she could bear it. Besides, she remembered with a start, Shahnawaz was coming.

"Calm down, Peter," she said. "I think it's better if you don't come right now. I'm just going to take a cab home and curl up in bed; I'm really, really tired."

To her surprise and relief, he did not insist.

"Okay," he said curtly. "I'll leave you alone if that's what you want."

"I just need a couple of days to process things," she said, the reality of the accident and the hospital weighing on her. "It's almost Christmas, and I have to go and deal with my family. You know how hard that is for me. Maybe we can talk tomorrow." There was an awkward silence. She felt as if she were talking to a stranger.

"Okay, if that's the way you want it," Peter said, and hung up.

She held the phone away from her cheek, as if she had been slapped. *Did he hang up on me?* she thought. And then, almost immediately: *I didn't have to be so mean to him. He's upset about something.*

She felt an almost physical sensation of guilt. She lay back on the hard hospital pillow and closed her eyes. A mist of sleep was settling over her when voices pulled her back to reality. She sat up to find the nurse standing in the doorway, talking over her shoulder to someone in the hall.

The nurse stepped back, apparently in deference to an important guest.

"Here is the lady you are looking for," she announced. She held out her arm as if announcing a celebrity. "Claire Harris!"

Behind her stood Shahnawaz, beaming. He held an enormous bouquet of red roses. Claire had never seen so many flowers together in one bunch.

"Get well soon, Claire." He handed her the bouquet. She needed two hands to hold it.

"Oh, Shahnawaz," she said, joyful to see him. "How beautiful! Thank you so much!"

"Wait," she added to the nurse, who was halfway out of the door. "Do you have something I can put these in, please?"

The nurse beamed. "Of course, honey, I'll see what I can find," she said, and disappeared.

There was a chair beside the window. Shahnawaz placed it as near as he could to the head of the bed, and sat down. Claire told him everything she could remember about the accident.

"There is too much drinking and driving in this country," he said, almost to himself, frowning. Then he looked into her eyes. "You should have listened to your instincts," he continued, sounding very serious, "and made David find a cab to take you both home. It is most important to take care of yourself." Claire was touched and amused by his concern.

"Are the doctors sure you are perfectly all right?" he continued. There are no internal injuries?"

"Oh no, I am fine. In fact, they're sending me home this evening."

"That is wonderful. What time will you be discharged? I will come and see you home."

"I am fine, really. I can take a cab." Claire said. It felt like a betrayal to allow Shahnawaz come to get her when she had told Peter not to.

"It would be my pleasure to see you home safely. Please."

"If that's what you want," said Claire, feeling that, at least, it was what she wanted. "Don't worry. I won't go anywhere without you." She smiled.

"And how is your friend, the driver?" He sounded genuinely interested.

"David has a concussion, I think. They're keeping him another night in the hospital. I must go and stick my head in his room."

"Please tell him that I wish him a speedy recovery."

"Of course," said Claire. "I'm sure he will be grateful."

* * *

Claire listened to Shahnawaz's footsteps fade. Somehow, her headache didn't seem as bad as before.

Peter was worried about me too. But I just felt annoyed. Why does this man make me feel better? For some reason, she felt ridiculously happy.

She got out of bed, slipped on the strange shapeless socks she found in her bed table drawer, and went down the hall to Room 608.

David lay flat on the bed with a brace on his neck and his eyes closed. After a few seconds, he opened his eyes and tried to turn his head to look at her. He gave a low groan.

"Don't try to move, David," said Claire, coming to the end of the bed so he could see her more easily. "Do you need a painkiller or something? The nurse is really sweet. Do you want me to call her?"

"Oh, Claire," he said. "You were right. We should have taken a cab. I'm such an idiot."

"Forget it, David. It wasn't your fault. Really. The guy hit you."

"Are you okay?"

"Yeah, I think so. My head hurts a little. Would you like me to find you a cup of tea or something?"

"God, no. Nothing to eat or drink. Mainly, I don't want to move my head. It was all those margaritas. Or maybe the vodka shots. "

"Maybe. They'll be out of your system soon. But it's probably the concussion that's bothering you. I'm sure you'll feel better tomorrow. I think they want you to stay another night."

"What about you?"

"I'm getting out this evening. A friend is coming to pick me up." She didn't want to explain about Shahnawaz. "Do you want me to call your parents or someone?"

"No, Claire. Please. I can't deal with my parents right now. My mother will get hysterical. Today is Sunday. No one will miss me. I'll call them myself tomorrow. Right now, I don't really want to talk to anyone." He put his hands over his eyes.

"I understand," said Claire. She bent over and kissed him on top of the head. "Take care, David. Get some rest. I'll talk to you tomorrow."

* * *

When Shahnawaz arrived, the doctor had already signed Claire's discharge papers. The blouse she had worn on her way to the party had been crushed at the bottom of her bag. Feeling a little silly, she had put on the red sequined top again. She was ready to go.

"You look much better," he said. "I have never seen you like this," he added. "In fact, if you don't mind me saying so, you look very beautiful."

"Perhaps I should be admitted to the hospital more often," she replied, smiling. "To be truthful, I don't always dress this way on Sunday afternoons."

Shahnawaz helped her on with her coat, and went to get the car. The jovial nurse appeared with a wheelchair and insisted on taking her down to the lobby. She felt foolish sitting there, her lap full of roses. An array of humanity milled about the lobby, many looking anxious or bored. A small child skipped around the chairs as if she were in a playground. No one paid the slightest attention. The child's mother was on her cell phone.

A man with one leg passed Claire on crutches slowly, apparently in pain. She thought immediately of Luke, then of Peter's anger and bitterness. How terrible that he had to return so soon to Afghanistan, risking death or injury, perhaps returning more alienated than ever. He must be afraid too. A wave of guilt washed over her. The sensation was becoming oddly familiar. Here she was, waiting for Shahnawaz. Still, she cared for Peter deeply. She felt tired and confused – and glad that she didn't have to deal with him at the moment.

Then she saw the tall Afghan through the window, striding towards the hospital entrance, eager to take care of her when she needed it. She wondered what terrible things he himself might have gone through in the far-off country that was his home. How strange that he should be the one coming to pick her up.

A moment later, he was beside her, taking the flowers and helping her to her feet. She caught her breath for a moment as she sank into the leather seat of the BMW. *Clearly,* she thought, *he is doing well in this country.*

"What do they say? I will give you a penny for your thoughts," said Shahnawaz, and smiled. "Do I have it right?"

"I was just thinking about the state of the world, I guess."

"Ah yes," said Shahnawaz, pulling out into the traffic. "The world. Not a kind nor a just place, I fear."

"Still," she replied, putting her hand on the dashboard, "it has treated you well, it seems."

"Oh," said Shahnawaz. He paused. "If only you knew."

"But there is no need to think of that right now," he continued, his voice sounding oddly sad and distant. He turned and looked at her. "And where are we going?"

"Oh, I'm sorry." She gave her address.

"What block are you on? That number is on the south side, isn't it?"

The car purred like a satisfied cat. The windows were closed, shielding them from the noise on First Avenue. They drove for a while in silence.

"Do you live with your parents?" asked Shahnawaz.

"Oh no, I live alone. My parents are on Long Island. It's a long commute. I'm too old to be living with them anyway. I love having my own apartment."

"Do you see them often?"

"You ask a lot of questions, don't you?"

"I'm sorry, I don't mean to be rude."

"Oh no, it's fine. Just surprising." She paused. "Well, I see them pretty often."

Immediately, she regretted misleading him. In fact, she hardly ever saw her parents. They had been divorced for fifteen years. Her father had moved to London, and her mother remarried soon afterwards. She had gained a sister, an older brother, and a stepfather who seemed less than interested in his new, resentful teenage daughter. She didn't like him either. But Afghans, she assumed, were family oriented. For some reason, she didn't want Shahnawaz to think that she didn't care.

The rush hour traffic slowed them, but it didn't take long to reach her apartment.

"Here we are, then," announced Shahnawaz, pulling up in front of her canopy.

"Would you like to come up for some coffee?" Claire asked politely. He had done so much for her today; it was the least she could do. "Or tea? Or a glass of wine maybe?"

He hesitated. "Of course," he said rather stiffly. "Tea would be delightful."

By some miracle, there was a parking space just a few cars down. He pulled into it effortlessly and came around to open the door for her. He helped her out and took the flowers.

Claire's apartment was on the seventh floor. She unlocked the door while Shahnawaz fumbled with the flowers and made a valiant effort to open it for her. The air was filled with the smell of roses.

"Thank you. I can do it," she said, smiling.

The door opened almost directly into the living room, a small room with one big window looking out on a jumble of rooftops, a sleek slice of the United Nations building, and beyond, the East River and the 59th Street Bridge.

"I love the view," said Claire. "Sit down and relax. I'll take those. They need to be in water." She stepped into the tidy kitchen, put on the kettle, and found a vase and a hand-glazed pitcher. There was nothing large enough to hold all the roses. One of the blossoms had snapped off. She balanced it in a juice glass, and brought it back to the living room.

Shahnawaz was still standing.

"Please, let me make some tea for both of us."

"Don't be silly," said Claire. "Have a seat. It will only take a minute."

"No, no, you must rest; you have been in the hospital."

"I am fine," she said again, but Shahnawaz was adamant. She was pleased and touched by his determination.

"I am here to make sure that you are all right. Now, where do you keep your tea?" he added, moving into the kitchen.

In the tiny space, he looked even taller. She stepped back and pointed to the cabinet over the sink.

"In there," she said, catching her breath. In fact, she did feel a bit shaky. Her heart was pumping hard. It occurred to her that maybe she should sit down.

"Thank you. Now, you must be the one to relax and get comfortable. I will make the tea and bring it to you."

"Whatever you say," Claire said and retreated to the living room. There didn't seem to be a choice.

She sat quietly and concentrated on the single rose. It was half open – beautiful, but tentative. She hoped it would reach full bloom.

A few minutes later, Shahnawaz appeared holding a tray with two mugs of steaming tea and a plate of cookies. He put the tray on the table and handed Claire a mug, careful to turn the handle so that she would not burn herself. She felt taken care of.

Shahnawaz settled into the old armchair beside the couch, leaning forward as he talked to her.

"After Christmas," he said, "I will take you to that Afghan restaurant as I promised; this week, you must rest."

"Maybe you're right. It was a long night. I do feel tired. It's strange, but it feels like the whole thing happened a long time ago."

They chatted as they drank their tea. It was all so easy.

When Shahnawaz got up to go, Claire rose too. He stepped forward and reached out a hand to help her, but when she stood, he did not let go. They were standing very close. She looked up at him and their eyes met. He put his hands on her arms and pulled her gently towards him. She shivered but said nothing. He looked into her eyes as if searching for something. She felt hypnotized by his gaze. He was shivering too. He pulled her closer, bent down, and kissed her softly. Then she was kissing him back, passionately, and time stood still. The small living room seemed to blur around them; there was nothing for either of them but this moment.

They stood there kissing for what seemed a long time. Instinctively, Claire slid her arms around his back and pushed her body against him.

Shahnawaz stiffened and pulled back.

"Oh, God! What has come over me? I am so sorry."

"Sorry?" she said, confused. "Don't be sorry." Then she thought about Peter, and stepped back too.

"I must be mad. I am acting like a love-starved teenager," he continued, shaking his head and looking at the floor. "I came here to make sure you were okay, and that you reached your apartment safely. I had no right to encroach on your privacy."

"My privacy? Oh no." She wasn't sure what distressed him, or why he had pulled away. *Oh dear,* she thought, *he must think that I act this way with everyone.* She wanted desperately to make him feel better. "Please don't worry," she said, "it was my fault too."

"No, I should not have kissed you; this will not happen again," he said.

"Don't worry, please," she repeated. "We are friends, aren't we? It was just a kiss. Nothing really happened."

"Of course," he said, sounding unsure. "You are completely right. It was nothing." He walked over and took his coat from the hook by the door.

"I am so sorry. I really must go," he said. In a moment, he was gone.

Claire felt drained. It had all seemed so natural. But Shahnawaz was clearly upset. And there was Peter, of course. She was upset too.

She took off her glittery top and heels and stood for a long time under a hot shower. Afterwards, she felt better. She put on her night shirt and curled up on the sofa, mulling over her strange time with this ridiculously handsome man. She didn't understand why Shahnawaz was fighting this undeniable attraction. But she understood her own hesitations. Peter, Peter, Peter. They had been together forever. They were going to get married. Everyone knew. But right now, she didn't feel that she knew anything anymore; she didn't want to think about any of it.

* * *

Shahnawaz pulled his car out into the December darkness, his mind and body buzzing with emotion. For all these years in New York he had kept himself apart. Occasionally, at a business party or social event, he had flirted with an American woman. Once, briefly, he had bedded one. But he had not touched another woman with heartfelt passion since the death of his beloved Sara. In Afghan culture, a man was not supposed to touch a woman that way before marriage. But he felt helpless when he was with Claire. The rules he knew so well no longer seemed to apply. He felt both lost and found.

When he reached his building, he sat in the car for a few minutes, collecting himself. Then he turned over the keys to the attendant, stepped into the marble lobby, and the shining mirrored elevator carried him skyward to his apartment.

Chapter Seven

CB

David was discharged the next day from the hospital, shaken and ashamed, with a stiff neck and a terrible headache. Soon, everyone knew about the accident. When friends called to ask about his health, he told them about Claire, and she was bombarded with calls and texts from well-wishers too.

* * *

Christmas came with astonishing speed. New York wore its usual holiday finery: a giant star dangled over the intersection of 57th Street and 5th Avenue. Tourists gawked at Rockefeller Center's majestic Christmas tree. But the decorations festooning the city no longer delighted – they had been there for over a month already, and time was marching on.

Claire spent an uncomfortable Christmas day with her family – she didn't tell them about the accident. Her friends were all with their relatives. It seemed better than staying alone.

She steeled herself as she rang the bell of the neat

suburban Long Island house where her mother and stepfather Jonathan lived, eyeing the inflatable snow man in the front yard with dismay. Jonathan's taste had clearly trumped her mother's. Her mother hugged her tight, and she air kissed Jonathan with a strained smile. By now, everyone understood their antipathy – and the truce they observed at family events.

She disappeared as quickly as she could into the kitchen to help out. It was best to stay busy. After dinner, there was nothing left to do but settle into the living room and open presents she didn't want, from people who knew nothing about her taste and preferences, under the glare of a Christmas tree festooned with bubbling candle lights in many colors. Claire remembered Christmas before her parents' divorce, when tiny white lights had dotted the tree like stars. She felt assaulted. She focused on the crackling fire.

"How's the job?" Jonathan asked.

"Oh, it's all right," Claire replied. "It's an easy walk to the subway."

"How about Peter?" added her mother, who always said what was on her mind.

"He's fine," she said. "But he's not looking forward to going back overseas. He hates the whole situation in Afghanistan."

"Are you getting engaged before he leaves? Or waiting till he comes home?" She wished her mother would stop asking questions.

"Things are kind of up in the air right now. We're putting off the engagement for a while."

Suddenly, the idea of marrying Peter seemed outrageous to her. She could not imagine it happening. She saw the handsome face of Shahnawaz in her mind.

This is insane, she thought. *Every time Peter comes up, I think about a man I hardly know.* She couldn't wait to get back to her apartment.

* * *

Peter spent a quiet Christmas at home with his parents and sister, people who cared deeply for him. On Christmas Eve, he dreamt about sitting across from Luke, the old Luke, cracking jokes, looking perfectly normal. Luke's laugh was booming, then the sound morphed into distant explosions and the air in the room began to vibrate. Peter looked down at Luke's legs as they slowly dissolved into thin air. "I'm feeling just great," said dream Luke, smiling.

Peter sat up with a start. The shadow of Afghanistan was already darkening his mind.

His mother called from downstairs, and he descended into the warmth of his family and joyous traditions – the strains of Handel's Messiah and Christmas carols, silly Christmas stockings, roast turkey and plum pudding with brandy butter. No one mentioned his imminent departure. He felt in a bubble, detached from his family's determined Christmas cheer – and sad that he and Claire had argued. He called her, and they agreed to have dinner the night before his leave was up. But the conversation was short, almost forced. His mind kept drifting to Afghanistan. He felt as if he had nothing to say.

He sat on his bed and thought about this war which had no end in sight; about everyday life fraught with anxiety and danger. New Yorkers had endured the catastrophe of the World Trade Center, but they had no clue about life in Afghanistan, where constant vigilance was imperative. Attacks were swift, sudden, and totally unpredictable. An Afghan who seemed friendly one day, might turn out to be a deadly enemy tomorrow. The Taliban materialized from nowhere, and vanished as quickly, blending with innocent villagers or disappearing into the barren countryside, a land as hostile as its people. Since Luke's maiming in the I.E.D. incident, Peter had hated every day there. But now, he would return. He had no choice. Besides, his men were waiting.

* * *

In a flash, Christmas was over, and Peter's leave was almost up. He called Claire to remind her about dinner.

"Oh Peter, I can't believe it," she said. "We've hardly seen each other, and now it's time for you to go. I can't bear the idea that you will be in danger so soon."

"Me neither," he said. "So it goes." There was a pause.

"Listen, Claire, we are getting together tonight, right? Tomorrow, I report to my unit. Then I'll be gone."

"Of course, Peter. It will be good to see you. I've been thinking about you a lot." She really meant it.

"OK. I'll be at your place about seven. We'll decide where to go when I get there."

"Yes," said Claire, "We need to talk."

She hung up, and the phone started ringing again immediately.

Maybe Peter forgot something, she thought. But when she answered, it was Shahnawaz.

"Hello Claire," he said.

"Hello," said Claire. His voice produced a physical sensation.

Oh God, she thought, panicked, *this is so wrong. What will I feel when I actually see him?*

"Now Christmas is over, I thought tonight might be a good time for that Afghan dinner I promised you." He sounded a bit distant and formal. "I know this is last minute. I hope you don't mind."

She didn't mind, of course. But she was committed to dinner already. Her heart sank at the thought of having to refuse Shahnawaz again.

"I can't, Shahnawaz. I have to see Peter tonight – he is leaving for Kabul tomorrow. We've had this set up for a while. I am so, so sorry."

"Oh," said Shahnawaz, taken aback. Somehow, he had assumed that Claire would accept. *Maybe*, he thought, *this lovely girl has thoughts only for Peter. Or maybe she is reacting to my inappropriate behavior.* He paused for a moment, and Claire jumped in.

"We can go another time, can't we?"

"Yes. Of course. Another time, I will certainly give you more notice. Goodbye. I am so sorry." He hung up feeling awkward, a sensation he was not used to. He did not like it at all.

Claire gasped. For a moment, she stared at the phone in her hand as if she expected it to explain what had happened. *He is angry*, she thought. *Maybe I've driven him away. What if he doesn't call?*

She felt at a loss. She had to have dinner with Peter, of course. They had been together for so long, and she wouldn't see him for a whole year. Things had not been easy since his return, but she felt that they would work things out. It seemed crazy to feel so bad about turning down this one invitation.

Still, it was the second time she had refused Shahnawaz. She felt an inexplicable bond with this Afghan. She did not want to lose it.

After Peter leaves, she thought, *I'll call and apologize.*

Then she turned her thoughts to this last special evening.

* * *

Precisely at seven, Peter rang the bell.

"Hello Peter," said Claire, smiling.

"Hi babe," he said, noting the curves of her body under the filmy blouse, and gold hoop earrings glinting in the heavy waves of her hair. "I can never believe how gorgeous you are. I should go AWOL and just stay here with you forever."

"Do that," she said, laughing. Then she stopped for a moment, remembering how, after they had seen Luke at the hospital, she had begged him to leave the service. *It's his last night,* she reminded herself, making herself smile up at him again. "Then they can send me to prison after they track you down, and we'll snuggle together in our cell."

They continued their banter on the way to the restaurant. He put his arm around her as they walked, and she felt safe. After a couple of drinks, they ordered food. But by the time it came, they were quieter. Time was short; it was impossible to avoid real discussion any longer.

"I've been thinking a lot, Claire," said Peter suddenly. "There's something I need to tell you before I go."

Claire looked at him, then down at her food. *I don't want to hear this*, she thought.

"If something happens to me over there, don't let yourself shut down. You need to stay open to things, lead a normal life – find someone else and marry him."

"Don't be ridiculous, Peter," Claire said, sounding irritated. She was worried that she would start to cry. "You are coming back and we'll get engaged and everything will work out fine."

"Listen," said Peter, reaching out his hands and taking hers. "Things happen. Look at Luke. You have to be ready to forget me. That's what will keep me going."

"Stop talking like this," said Claire. "You will come back. This crazy war will be over soon. Let's talk about good things – the good times are what I want to hang onto."

"No, babe," said Peter, squeezing her hands a bit tighter than was comfortable. His blue eyes were very serious. "I need you to promise me."

The intensity of his gaze was too much – again, this was a Peter she hardly recognized. She wanted desperately to change the subject. Bizarrely, she felt compelled to tell him about Shahnawaz's call.

"Here's something weird, Peter," she said, as if starting in on some entertaining story. "That Afghan we met in the restaurant keeps asking me out to dinner."

"What?" said Peter, his intense gaze shifting to a frown. "I thought you had just run into him."

"Well I did. He works really near me."

"So you gave him your cell number when you met him on the street? That's a creepy thing to do. What were you thinking?"

Claire felt defensive. For herself, and for Shahnawaz too, almost as if she needed to protect him. "As a matter of fact, I did. He wanted to make up for being rude. He was just being polite."

"I bet," said Peter and let go of her hands. He picked at the edge of his thumbnail with his index finger.

For a little while, neither spoke. Claire pushed her salad around with her fork while Peter stared at her. He took a deep breath, and rubbed his mouth with one hand, shaking his head as if saying no. Then he signaled to the waiter to pour more wine.

"Sorry, babe. It's just that we need to keep things real. It's another world over there. Death is in the air. Suffering. You're either bored or scared out of your mind. But you learn to live with it. I don't know how to explain it to you."

Claire said nothing. She wanted to offer support and reassurance. But she didn't know what to say. Afghanistan seemed so far away – how could she ever understand what he was going through? She felt anxious and distant, the way she had after their first wonderful dinner together. As if he were already gone.

"You will be fine, Peter," she said. "I know you will be fine." Even to herself, she sounded unsure.

It wasn't the same after that. When their coffee came, Peter ordered a shot of brandy. He drank it in a single gulp.

"I am tired, Claire," he said. "And I have to get my stuff together. I'm going to take you home."

They held hands in the cab, and she rested her head on his shoulder. When they reached her apartment building, he gave her a quick kiss, then held her so hard she couldn't get her breath and had to pull away from him.

"It'll be okay, Peter," she said, holding him at arm's length.

"I know," he said. He let go of her and slid back into the cab. "Be good, babe," he said, and pulled the door shut behind him.

"Goodbye, Peter," she said. She had never felt sadder. "I'll be thinking of you." That, at least, was true.

* * *

At 7 am the next morning, Peter flew to Baltimore for deployment. By two that afternoon, he was on an army transport jet. Almost 15 hours later, he was flying over rugged brown mountains streaked with snow. They landed heavily, the belly of the plane opened and he stepped out into cold dry air and a swirl of dust: Afghanistan was waiting.

Chapter Eight

C３

The past was shadowing Shahnawaz again. After meeting Claire, his spirits had brightened, life seemed a little easier, his pain less severe. He had been eager to cultivate their friendship. But then, she had refused to see him – not once but twice – and the more he thought about her behavior, the more unsettled he became.

Perhaps she does not like me, he thought. *No, she can't even tolerate me.* The idea was such a blow to his self-esteem that he did not know how to handle it. *Only a fool would keep asking her out. I will not ask again.*

He did his best to go on with his life as always, but Claire's face kept popping into his mind's eye – on a conference call, signing papers, driving his car.

He chastised himself quietly most of the time. But once, when he was alone, he shouted, "What is wrong with me!" as if verbal self-rebuke would make a difference.

Indeed, as time passed, he did not think of her quite so often.

But as Claire's brightness faded, the past rose to fill the

present. He thought again and again of what he had lost – the devotion of his parents; his wife's sad dark eyes; his daughter's rosy cheeks even as she lay dead in his arms. When these ghosts came to haunt him, the flicker of hope Claire had sparked in him seemed gone.

Slowly, his brother Rubnawaz came to dominate his musings. Rubnawaz, nine years his junior – little Raby once, an intense, tousled, passionate child who begged for rides on his back, then tried to stand on his shoulders. Raby, who begged for his attention, whom he taught to fly a kite, running again and again and again, tangled in the string, until his little dark face was bathed in sweat, and when Shahnawaz laughed and told him to stop, just kept on running until the kite finally rose and, wondrously, caught the air, soaring higher and higher. Raby, who worshipped him.

Shahnawaz had failed Raby too.

* * *

Raby was seventeen years old when tragedy struck their family. In Pakistan, as the weeks dragged by, Shahnawaz thought hard about the practicalities of revenge, forcing himself to temper his anger towards the Tabani. But Raby's hatred festered within him. It grew and grew.

"I know you believe in waiting, Lala," he declared one evening in Pakistan, using the honorific for an older brother. "But I will not wait. And you will not have to either. I will take the revenge."

"No, Raby. You must not let hatred cloud your future. It was my men who killed the Tabani. It is my fault that we have lost all we loved. It is my responsibility."

"No, Lala! You were only obeying orders; the Tabani

knew that you had no ill will. If our enemies are cruel and unreasoning, they deserve the same. Let us pay them in their own coin. I will do it. I am not afraid."

"Fear has nothing to do with it, Raby. We have not left our country out of cowardice. It is a question of strategy. We have saved ourselves so that we can take revenge." He paused. "There will be a time. But for now, we must wait."

But Raby was adamant. His parents had doted on this son of their older years. When Shahnawaz had enlisted, their mother smothered her youngest with love – even his reserved and dignified father had been very affectionate. It was his duty, he felt, to kill those who had destroyed this loving family, and with them, his entire life.

"I will do what must be done," he declared, his chin high, staring directly at his brother. "No matter what – or who – stands in my way."

"Raby, now that our father is gone, I must act as your father. You must listen to me and not do anything foolish."

"But you are too rational to do real harm to our enemies, Lala. I know it. I see you getting soft. You would take them to court, make them bend to the laws of the land. But they are beasts and should be treated accordingly."

Shahnawaz sighed. "I understand, Raby. But promise me something. Keep your options open. We will discuss it further. That is my promise."

"Yes Lala, I promise," said Raby, his eyes pools of darkness.

Shahnawaz did not believe him. He knew how stubborn his little brother was.

Still, life moved on as always, and the brothers found themselves settling into the ways of Peshawar.

* * *

Rubnawaz spoke on the phone often to his friend Shahid, Commander Akbar's son. Shahid told Raby of the dangers he and his family were facing.

"The other day they fired bullets at our car," he said proudly, as if he were boasting. "It is not easy fearing for your life, always looking over your shoulder. You are lucky you went to Pakistan, Raby."

"Yes," said Rubnawaz. He did not feel lucky at all.

These conversations stoked Raby's anger. The places and the people he knew were where they had always been. For Shahid, little had changed. But Raby saw the world differently now – warped by his hatred of the Tabani.

* * *

Sabir Khan had helped Shahnawaz and Raby find jobs in different areas of Peshawar. Shahnawaz worked in an elegant men's clothing shop virtually indistinguishable from one in Kabul. But Raby went every day to the outskirts of the city, a lawless area controlled by tribal lords who only pretended allegiance to the Pakistani government. Criminal groups ruled the streets. They hijacked cars, and kidnapped the rich and held them for ransom. And if their demands were not met, they did not hesitate to cut off an ear, or dump a body beside the road. The practice was very profitable. Raby feared them. Still, he dreamed of hiring them to murder the Tabani.

One day, over a simple lunch in the shade of a lone banyan tree, Raby told his family's tragic story to a fellow worker named Rafeeq. As he spoke, he dug his nails into his palm, and his eyes filled with passionate tears.

"These are terrible things," Rafeeq said. "Why don't you do

something? Do you not burn inside to teach these people a lesson?"

"I can think of nothing else," said Raby through clenched teeth. "But what can I do? They are across the border, and I am helpless."

"Maybe not," said Rafeeq. He paused and stared into the distance, over Raby's shoulder. "I may be able to introduce you to a man who can help."

"You can? You must take me to him now!"

"It is not that simple, my friend. I must ask this man's permission to bring you to his home. He is a powerful person."

"Okay, okay, Rafeeq. But contact him, please. I must see him at any cost."

"I will see what I can do. But when we take you to his place, you will be blindfolded."

"It does not matter." It seemed a minor inconvenience.

Raby mentioned nothing about the meeting to Shahnawaz. He knew his brother would forbid him to go.

As he waited, his obsession with revenge grew. He slept little, and when he did, what had once been restless dreams turned to horrifying nightmares. He lay staring into the darkness, determined not to wake his brother.

A few days later, Rafeeq brought news. The important man had given permission for a meeting. Raby was elated. He did not ask the man's name.

"I will pick you up here at ten. You must be waiting."

"Thank you, Rafeeq," said Raby. He could feel his excitement mounting. "You are truly a friend."

Rafeeq came in the back of a car with tinted windows. The driver pulled over, Rafeeq pushed open the door, and Raby got in. His friend tied a blindfold over his eyes. They drove for what seemed like a long time. No one spoke. Raby felt the car stop and heard a gate creak open. The driver spoke through the window to someone in a low voice, and the car moved ahead slowly, pulling around as if circling a driveway. Rafeeq helped him out, and there was more whispered conversation. A door opened, and Rafeeq guided Raby in.

"Be respectful," Rafeeq said in a low, clipped voice. They turned to the left and walked a few steps further. Then Raby felt a hand on his shoulder, pressing him downwards. He felt himself sit on a cushioned surface.

"Remove the blindfold," said Rafeeq into his ear. Raby pulled up the cloth, opened his eyes, blinked, and looked around.

He had been in darkness for a long time.

He was sitting on a low sofa in a large room with a rich red rug on the floor. Opposite him, on a grand upholstered armchair sat a middle aged man with a long beard and narrow eyes. Raby took an instant dislike to him. But that did not matter. The man was offering him a golden opportunity.

A servant arrived with a tray of tea, the traditional refreshment for any guest.

"Drink," said the man. "You are welcome in my home."

They drank in silence. Then, the man asked Raby to tell his story.

"So," said the man, "You are eager to avenge your family?"

"I can think of nothing else."

"I can help you achieve your goal. But this achievement requires great sacrifice. Are you ready for that?"

"Yes, I am ready."

"You must do the killing yourself."

"But how?" Raby asked.

"We will provide you with the means. And we will take you to him. Then, all you have to do is pull a string, and it will be over."

It took a second for Raby to take in what the man was saying. Then, his eyes widened.

"You want me to wear explosives. I will be killed too."

"As I said," said the man calmly. "Great sacrifice. Not to be taken lightly. Go now, and think about this carefully. When you know that you are ready, Rafeeq will bring you back to me, and we will start your training."

"Yes," said Raby, frowning. He found himself clenching his jaw.

"One more thing: you must not discuss what we have talked about here. Not with your brother. Not with anyone. Or there will be consequences. Am I clear?"

"Yes, sir. I understand."

Rafeeq handed Raby the blindfold, and the process was repeated.

In the car, thoughts swirled through Raby's head. The death of his enemies had been paramount in his mind. He had never thought about his own.

* * *

Just as Raby spoke to his friend Shahid, Shahnawaz remained in touch with his comrade Jamshed. Jamshed told him that he had been designated a deserter, and would face court-martial if he ever returned to Afghanistan.

Meanwhile, Jamshed said, the Tabani had carried out another attack on Commander Akbar. This time, Akbar had gotten a bullet in the arm; his guard and driver had been killed.

"Negotiations with the Tabani have failed completely. Akbar agrees they must be stopped," Jamshed told Shahnawaz on the phone.

"Yes," said Shahnawaz. "Tariq Tabani will not compromise his honor."

"My only solace," his friend continued, "is that you are out of harm's way."

"I find no solace in that fact, Jamshed. If I had stayed, I could have taken my revenge."

"I disagree. Tabani is obsessed with his hatred for you. He would have tried to kill you again and again. And he would have succeeded."

"So you have told me," Shahnawaz replied.

But Shahnawaz did find comfort in one thing – his little brother's safety. Nonetheless, he worried about Raby. The boy was silent much of the time, brooding. Once, he had been a dedicated student, planning to become a doctor. In Peshawar, that dream lay shattered. As a refugee, his education was over. The future was bleak.

* * *

After meeting the mysterious man, Raby wanted desperately to discuss the situation with Shahnawaz. But he knew what his brother would say, and he could not bear to go against him. In spite of his stubborn nature, he had always yielded to authority. But the family tragedy had forced him into manhood. He might break his promise to keep his options open, but the decision would be his own.

A week later, Raby informed Rafeeq that he was ready to go for training. He told Shahnawaz that he had been invited to spend time with a cousin in Rawalpindi. Shahnawaz was surprised, but pleased that Raby seemed to be coming out of his shell.

In fact, Raby was taken to a remote hilly place in the tribal region of Waziristan. After ten days, he returned, his training completed. He would be called and taken to carry out his mission.

When Raby asked why this stranger was helping him, Rafeeq told him that the man himself had a grudge against the Tabani. Raby was a convenient means to take revenge with impunity. Raby was not happy with this. He wanted revenge to be his alone. But this was his only chance to get back to Afghanistan. He was ready; the decision was final.

In the days after his training, Raby spent as much time with his brother as he could. For the first time in many months, he felt calm. Shahnawaz was pleased with his progress. When the call came, Raby wrote a letter to his brother and gave it to a trusted friend, with instructions to post it the following day:

```
Dear Lala,
    I am going to avenge our family. By the time
you receive this letter, I will have joined
our parents in heaven. I will bring them your
love, and tell your beloved wife and daughter
that someday you too will join us.
    Please Lala, do not mourn my death or cry
for me. I chose this. Every second since the
Tabani attack, I have yearned to take revenge.
    My dying wish is that you take no violent
action yourself. Swear it on our father's
grave. Let mine be the final word.
```

Take care of yourself, and Allah be with
you.

No one could ask for a more worthy brother.

Goodbye.

Raby

* * *

After what seemed like an endless journey, Raby found himself
once more in Kabul. It was evening now. The car pulled up on
a side street. He could hear voices nearby and music – sounds
of a Tabani wedding for a cousin of Tariq Tabani.

"The enemy is around the corner," said Rafeeq. "Go in,
find Tabani's son and take your revenge. Allah be with you."

"Yes," said Raby, hearing his own voice far away. "It is
time." He got out of the car, blinking in the light. His legs felt
weak beneath him. As he walked towards the wedding tent,
he could feel his heart beating faster and faster.

A few guests were standing outside the entrance, talking.
They smiled and nodded as he walked between them, and
he nodded back. There was a sharp noise inside, perhaps a
glass breaking, and all of a sudden, he saw his father in his
mind's eye, shot down in front of him. The weakness he had
felt before was washed away by a surge of anger. His legs
steadied as he moved forward. He felt completely focused and
electrically alive.

At the far end of the tent was a raised stage, where the
bride and groom sat on a lavish couch, greeting their guests.
Raby made his way towards them, scanning the crowd. At the
edge of the platform, he spotted Tabani's eldest son Shafeeq.
Raby had studied photographs of him. The young man was

laughing, surrounded by friends, but to Raby, they were nothing but a blur. All he could see was Shafeeq's gleaming smile.

All this time, he had thought he had understood true hatred. He had been wrong. This was what true hatred felt like. It burned.

He walked up and joined them.

"Hello Shafeeq," he said, putting out his hand.

"Hello," said Shafeeq politely and shook it. He frowned slightly, as if trying to recall Raby's face. There was no recognition in his eyes.

"I have brought you a present from my mother and father," said Raby. He reached under his tunic and grasped the string.

"*Allahu Akbar*," he cried as loud as he could. But his voice was drowned out by the explosion.

* * *

Raby's death was instantaneous. Shafeeq and two of his friends were blown to pieces. The stage collapsed, and twelve others were injured, including the bride and groom.

On the far side of the tent, Tariq Tabani staggered from the force of the blast. Only a few minutes earlier, his eldest son had taken his leave and gone to meet his friends near the wedding stage.

A wave of guests surged around the patriarch, fleeing for their lives, almost knocking him over. But he pushed his way through, calling Shareeq's name again and again, as if commanding his son to appear at his side. The tent smelled of smoke and flesh.

* * *

After the funeral, Tariq Tabani was a broken man. When Shahnawaz's rocket had killed his middle son, he had been filled with a righteous determination to mete out punishment. The attack, he knew, had been a mere error, yet he had exacted revenge and destroyed Shahnawaz's family. Now, two of his own three sons were gone. The last, only twelve years old, cried so much at the funeral that he vomited and had to be taken away to his mother. The family begged Tabani to stop the killings.

"It is enough," said Tariq Tabani. And his word was law.

* * *

Raby's letter to his brother arrived the next morning. But Shahnawaz was late for work, and waited to read it until he returned home that evening, tearing it open over a cup of tea. *Raby will no doubt be explaining his absence,* he thought, making himself comfortable on a cushion. *I must not be too hard on him.* He planned to temper his reaction. He understood his little brother's anguish and felt he deserved a break.

At work, someone had mentioned an explosion at a Tabani wedding, but he had not asked the details. He preferred not to think about the Tabani. Now, he understood.

The tea remained untouched

"Why, Raby? Why?" he cried, crushing the letter and throwing it from him, as if he could somehow obliterate what had happened. "Your whole life was in front of you!"

But he knew why, and his heart swelled with bitterness and shame. It was hard to breathe. *He told me,* he thought. *And I did not stop him. I am to blame. I failed him, as I failed my whole family.*

He stayed in his room for two days; crying and cursing himself. On the third day, there was a knock on the door.

"Shahnawaz?" He recognized the voice of his friend Jamshed, but he did not answer. The knocking got louder.

"Shahnawaz!" cried Jamshed. "Open the door!" He banged it with his fist twice, then waited.

"No. Leave me." Jamshed could barely hear him.

"Please Shahnawaz," said Jamshed. "I am not going anywhere. You must open the door."

Seconds ticked by, and the door opened a crack.

"Let me in, Shahnawaz. Please."

Shahnawaz stepped back to let him enter.

"I am most sorry about your brother," said Jamshed. "A terrible tragedy."

"It was my fault. Completely my fault. I did not realize…. I could not stop him." He fell to the floor and cried like a child, gasping for air between sobs, his shoulders shaking.

Jamshed stood in silence and waited. After some time, the sobs subsided, and Shahnawaz raised his head. Slowly, he got to his feet, and Jamshed put a hand on his shoulder.

"You cannot blame yourself, my friend. These boys have such passion. Who can know what they are thinking."

Shahnawaz rubbed his eyes with the heels of his hands and looked at Jamshed.

"Why have you come here?" he asked.

"I have brought you a message from Tariq Tabani."

"You have? The bastard. What does he want?"

"Raby's act has broken him, Shahnawaz. He wants peace; he wants to protect his family. He wants to put all this behind him."

"All right," said Shahnawaz. There seemed to be nothing else to say.

"There is no reason to live anymore," he added numbly. There were no more tears in him. "My brother, my parents, my wife and child – they are all dead. If I had not gone on that mission, they would be alive today."

"You did your duty," said Jamshed.

For an hour, they talked. Then Shahnawaz came out of his room and ate something.

"I cannot stay here," he told Jamshed. "I need to go where all this will no longer haunt me."

"You could go to America. I have a cousin in New York. And a person who can help you with a visa."

So it was settled. Jamshed took a few days leave and stayed in Peshawar, helping Shahnawaz make arrangements. He promised to liquidate the family assets on his return to Afghanistan and send his friend the money.

That was how Shahnawaz came to New York City. He had hoped to escape his misery. But his past traveled with him, of course.

Chapter Nine

℃ℨ

Claire was feeling guilty for refusing Shahnawaz's dinner invitation twice, but she could not muster the courage to call him. She was late for work again; and again, her supervisor was angry. She felt the threats were hollow. Still, it was a sour note to start the day.

She had always been a conscientious worker. But lately, she had been making stupid mistakes. Her heart was not in it. She needed to vent her frustration at this thankless job, but she felt she had no one to talk to. Peter was thousands of miles away; David would just shrug it off; it had been years since she'd confided in her mother. She regretted not making more female friends. But she preferred being around men anyway.

Shahnawaz, she thought. *I need to talk to Shahnawaz.*

The feeling of certainty was startling.

What if he hangs up on me? she thought. *Well if he does, I will least know the situation. I might as well do it now.*

She dialed his office.

"Hello?" His voice was unmistakable. He sounded distracted, as if interrupted in the middle of something. But her heart started pounding. She had expected an assistant to answer.

"I'd like to speak to Mr. Khan, please" she asked, buying time.

"Yes, speaking," he answered.

"This is Claire, Shahnawaz. I hope I'm not disturbing you. I just wanted to say hello." There was a pause.

"Oh, Claire," he said, his voice impersonal. "How are you?"

"I am fine." She had no idea what to say next. She felt panic rising. *I must be crazy,* she thought. *What was I thinking?*

"What can I do for you?" He sounded businesslike, a bit impatient, as if he were talking to a secondary client.

"Oh nothing, really," she said quickly, frightened by his tone. *Please God, do not let him hang up.* "I just wanted to say hello and see how you were doing." It sounded incredibly lame.

There was another, longer silence. For a moment, she thought he had cut her off.

"I am fine, Claire," he said finally. "But I must admit that I am surprised by your call. Frankly, I thought that you were annoyed by me asking you out again and again. That you preferred not to talk to me."

"Oh no, no, Shahnawaz," she said, more feeling in her voice than she had intended. But the words came out in a rush, from her heart, not her brain. "I am always happy to talk to you. I was just so busy when you called the other day. And the first time, I already had a commitment to Peter that I couldn't break. I thought you understood. It had nothing to do with my not wanting to see you. I did want to see you. I mean I do want to see you. I really do." She paused, wondering what she had just said, waiting for his reaction.

"All right, Claire, all right. It's all right. I believe you," he said, the familiar warmth flowing again into his voice. "But after you refused me twice, I decided not to impose myself on you again. That is why I have not called."

She felt wildly happy. She had not realized how much she had needed to talk to him. "I am so, so sorry," she said. "That was not what I meant at all." She felt instantly comfortable. It was ridiculously easy.

"Now, I think I should invite you somewhere – to make up for refusing you."

"Excellent," he said. "Where are you inviting me? And when, exactly?"

"There's a nice place near my office. We could have lunch tomorrow."

"I'll check my calendar."

The arrangements were made. Claire hung up smiling. Shahnawaz did too.

* * *

Peter found himself missing the States even before the plane touched down in Kabul. Like so many of his fellow soldiers, he was tired. The fighting had accomplished little. Now the American approach had shifted to support and persuasion, He was expected to win the respect and cooperation of these stubborn, resentful, independent people. He felt sorry for the Afghans, but he wished that this useless war was over.

Before his leave, he had been spent his days searching out roadside bombs and hidden attackers. This time, he was assigned to provide security for a girls' school on the edge of the city. His platoon secured the area around the school, creating a zone for parents, students and teachers safe from religious zealots determined that education be forbidden to girls.

His men patrolled on foot and in vehicles, at times even escorting the children.

Peter's jeep was parked on the edge of the road near the school, a patrol checkpoint. The children had already gone in, and he had a few minutes to look at some papers, while his driver took at catnap at the wheel. The man was supposed to stay alert, of course, but they'd been up since five, and things had been quiet. Peter didn't mind.

He sighed and looked up from his work, and there was the child, maybe 30 yards ahead of him, clearly late for classes, running along the road. She was alone, her books clasped to her chest, her white head scarf flapping behind her; each step of her small brown feet kicked up puffs of dust. She had nearly reached the school when a car drove up fast behind her. He could see that it was coming too quickly, but there was nothing he could do. As it was about to overtake her, she darted across the road in front of it. In a single motion, Peter yelled a warning, flung open the car door, and broke into a run.

There was a screech of brakes. The car swerved, skidded, and fishtailed, coming to a stop at a crazy angle. The girl lay unmoving, books scattered around her. A lone piece of paper floated to the ground.

Peter knelt beside the small body, afraid for a moment to touch her. The driver who had hit her appeared beside him, agitated, babbling in Pashto. Peter's driver came up behind him.

"Deal with this idiot, will you," said Peter. "I'll take her inside."

The child did not move. Peter lifted her carefully and walked slowly towards the school, doing his best not to jostle her. Her eyelids fluttered slightly. A young woman appeared and opened the gate. Peter did not take his eyes off the child.

"What happened?" asked the young woman, bending over the girl. "Is she all right?"

"She was hit by a car. My driver's got the man who hit her. Is there a place I can put her down? We should call an ambulance."

"Yes, of course. You can bring her in here." She ushered Peter past a reception area, through a cool hallway into a room with a few chairs and a sofa in one corner.

"It's for the staff," she explained, moving a pillow. Then she picked up a phone and gave some brief instructions.

Peter laid the girl down and she moaned softly. The woman returned and bent over the child again, stroking her forehead.

"It's all right, Fatima, it's all right," she said in Pashto. "Try to open your eyes."

The girl opened her eyes, closed them tight, then opened them again, even wider.

"Oh! Where am I?" she said, trying to sit up. She looked terrified.

"Keep still, little one. You will be fine, I promise." The young woman ran her hands softly over the small body. "Tell me if it hurts anywhere."

"No," said the girl. She tried to sit up again, then stopped and lay back down, her hands over her eyes. "My head," she said. Tears ran down her cheeks. The woman took her hand.

"Don't worry. The doctor will be here soon."

"The ambulance is on its way," she said to Peter over her

shoulder – in English now. "Thank you so much for bringing her in." She looked up at him for the first time.

"Oh no," Peter said, catching his breath. "Thank you."

She was so beautiful he could hardly speak. Her dark green hijab framed her face, setting off her golden skin and her wide, pale green eyes, the irises ringed with a dark circle. Her lips were full and slightly parted.

"Captain Peter Jenkins, United States Army," he continued stiffly, feeling awkward. "My unit is assigned to look after your school."

"I am Marriam," she said, looking at him quizzically. "I teach English literature to the higher classes." She extended an elegant hand, and he shook it with care, as if it were a precious object.

"I am so pleased to meet you," said Peter. The meaning of the polite words struck him for the very first time.

But there was no time to think. The room had filled with teachers, worried and wanting to know what happened. Peter and Marriam did their best to explain – then the ambulance pulled up outside.

"I will go with her," said Marriam firmly.

"Yes, of course," replied Peter. "I will accompany you. My driver can follow us."

In the ambulance, Marriam's eyes never left the child. The medic fussed with instruments and took readings, but Peter hardly noticed him. He was, however, acutely aware of sharing a small space with this strong, kind, beautiful teacher. Her presence filled his consciousness entirely. Walking behind her on the way to the ambulance, he had noticed her body moving beneath her long loose clothing – tall, slender and graceful.

He was determined to see her again. But how, once the injured girl was in the hospital?

"I am often on patrol often near your school," he said, doing his best to sound casual. "Do you think I could stop in sometime and ask how Fatima is doing?"

"Of course. You may have saved her life. You are welcome to come at any time."

"Terrific," said Peter, smiling. "I'll be sure to do that. Thank you."

The ambulance stopped and the doors opened. Their time together was over. Marriam went inside with the attendants; Peter climbed into the jeep. He was back on duty.

* * *

By early afternoon, Peter realized that any attempt to work was useless. All he could think of was Marriam. Unable to keep his mind focused – a key part of his job – he had his driver drop him off at the base. Almost no one was around. He went directly to the private room he enjoyed as an officer, turned on his computer, and sat on the chair at the small desk, lost in thought. Finally, he glanced at his emails. The first few were annoying announcements and promotions – one for life insurance – he gave a short laugh and deleted them without a second thought.

But the next email was from Claire. He hesitated before clicking on it, unsure if he wanted to read it right now. Claire's letters were as lively as her personality. This one, as always, was full of anecdotes, amusing things she had seen in the city, chatter about friends and colleagues. She mentioned Shahnawaz and his business briefly – as if he were a friend of Peter's too. At the end, she said how much she missed Peter, and asked him to tell her all about Afghanistan.

He clicked the email shut and frowned. He looked forward to Claire's emails. Sometimes, they made him ache with longing for her. Sometimes, they made him laugh. When she mentioned Shahnawaz, as she often did, he sometimes felt a pang of jealousy or a flash of irrational anger. Recently, the feelings had not been as intense as they had a few months ago. This time, he felt nothing at all.

What's wrong with me? he thought, switching off his computer. *Don't I love her anymore?*

He tried to summon Claire in his mind's eye, but all he could see was Marriam. Beautiful Marriam: her clear green eyes, her slender hands, her quiet voice. He wondered how long he had to wait before visiting the school.

Three days later, he felt it had been long enough. He had his driver park outside the school, and let himself in the gate. At the front desk, he asked to see Marriam, the English teacher.

"She is on leave today," said the receptionist. He gave Peter a hostile look.

Peter was astonished by the depth of his own disappointment.

"Will she be here tomorrow?" he asked, feeling as if something important had been taken from him.

"I don't know," replied the receptionist. This time, he did not even look up.

"How long is she on leave?" Peter said, determined to get an answer.

The secretary sounded angry. "I told you before, I don't know." He started typing something into his computer, as if the conversation was over.

"I don't understand," said Peter. "Why is she on leave? Is she sick?"

"She is not ill," said the secretary, looking up again. He stared at Peter as if he hated him. "She is with her family. Her oldest brother is dead. Murdered by allied forces."

"Oh God," said Peter, stunned. He stared at the secretary for a moment, then lowered his eyes. "That's terrible," he said, stepping back to the door. "I am so, so sorry."

He walked slowly back to his jeep, in a daze, overwhelmed by the hopelessness of his situation. Here he was, thousands of miles from home, trying to help people who did not want help at all. And he did not want to be here any more than they wanted him. The irony was overwhelming.

It's a miserable part of the world anyway, he thought. *Broiling in summer, freezing in winter.* He longed for the gentle pleasures of spring and fall back home. Safety, civilization, a temperate climate – these, he had thought, were all that he needed. But all of a sudden, now that he had met Marriam, he was no longer sure.

Any thoughts of befriending her, he knew, were wishful thinking. An American soldier could not be friends with a young Afghan woman. Besides, she must be devastated with grief at the death of her brother – and filled with hatred for those who had killed him. He drove back to camp, his brain buzzing with longing and uncertainty, which lasted long into a sleepless night.

* * *

In spite of all that his rational mind told him, Peter felt compelled to see Marriam again, to give her his condolences and assure her that he had not chosen this war. This time, he managed to stay away for almost a week. Then he drove back to the school, as if drawn by an invisible force.

He approached the receptionist politely, taking off his helmet, and asked to speak to the English teacher. The receptionist was a woman this time.

"What business do you have with her?" she asked curtly.

Peter hesitated. He had not expected to be questioned.

"There was a student – Fatima I think her name was. She was in an accident. I wanted to ask how she was doing."

"She is fine, I can assure you," said the receptionist. She looked up at Peter and raised an eyebrow, as if she suspected that was not why he wanted to see Marriam at all.

"Please, ma'am," he said urgently, "I need to speak to Miss Marriam. I really do." The receptionist gave him a searching look, nodded her head, and picked up the house phone. She spoke softly in Pashto, and Peter had no idea what she was saying, but he recognized Marriam's name – twice. She looked up at him again.

"Miss Marriam is in class now. She will not be free for another half hour. Would you like to make an appointment to see her another time?"

"No, no. I will wait. Please tell me where I can wait for her."

"There is a room at the end of the corridor, on the left, she said, gesturing. "You can wait there."

"Thank you," said Peter, feeling hugely relieved. "Thank you so much."

The waiting room was small, with portraits of Afghan heroes on the wall. He sat on a chair by the window and stared at them.

What in God's name am I going to say to this woman? he thought. *And why am I so desperate to see her anyway?*

The answer was shocking and instantaneous. *I want to see her because I need to see her. Not only see her, but be with her. She is all I can think about.*

He closed his eyes, attempting to absorb this amazing and terrible truth, struggling to calm himself with reason. But each time he told himself why this was impossible, the reality hit him with greater force: *I cannot live without her.*

He felt a presence in the room and opened his eyes. It was Marriam. She stood at the doorway, frowning slightly.

"Good morning," she said in her musical voice.

"Good morning," he replied automatically.

"I understand that you wish to see me?"

She did not move, as if she was ready turn on her heel at any moment and go back to her students.

"Come in and sit down," said Peter. "Please."

She looked surprised, but took a step into the room, perching on the edge of a chair opposite him.

Peter shuffled through his thoughts desperately, searching for something to say that would keep her from leaving.

"I came to ask about Fatima," he said finally. "I have no idea what happened after I left you with her at the hospital. Is she okay?"

Marriam looked relieved.

"Fatima is fine, thank you. She is back in school, and as late to class as ever." She smiled briefly. "I believe," she continued, "that she has learned from her experience. At least she looks both ways now before crossing the street."

"I am so glad to hear that," Peter said, trying his best to prolong the conversation. "I was worried about her. She seemed disoriented in the ambulance."

"I was relieved too." There was a silence. Peter could hear

his heart beating in his head. It sounded so loud that, for a moment, he worried that Marriam might hear it too. Marriam leaned forward, as if about to rise from her chair. This was his last chance to say something. He might never see her again.

The idea was unbearable.

"Actually," he blurted out. "It's not just Fatima. I mean, I did want to know how she was. But that wasn't all." He paused. *I have to say it*, he thought and looked deep into the green pools of her eyes.

"This is the truth," he continued quickly, so he would not have a chance to change his mind. "I came to talk to you. I needed to see you. I wanted to know you better." He paused again, registering the shock on her face. "That was why I came."

"What did you say?" said Marriam, standing up, her eyes as wide as a frightened deer's.

"I'm so sorry," he continued. The words were tumbling out now. He could not stop them. "I really don't know what is wrong with me. I can't sleep, I can't eat, I can't work. If I close my eyes for a second, all I see is your face. Your beautiful face." He looked up at her beseechingly, and saw that she was trembling, from shock, fear or bewilderment, he could not tell.

Then he saw the anger.

"You have no right to say these things to me," she said, fighting to control her voice. Her golden skin flushed with color. She clenched her notebook and pressed it to her chest, as if holding herself back from lashing out at him.

"I do not want to talk to you or see you again," she hissed. "Americans are our enemies. Don't you know that? You are invaders, and you have come to crush us. But you will not succeed. Kill as many as you want. You will not break us, no matter what you do." Her eyes were bright with defiance.

"No," said Peter, standing up too. He felt a surge of pride, and a burning desire to set the record straight. "You're wrong. That's not who we are. That's not who I am. We're not here to subjugate your people. We never were. We came to fight the terrorists. The terrorists who are your enemies as well as ours. The men who harm girls who wish to learn."

Marriam took a deep breath. "That is not the point," she said. "We do not care why you came. It is what you are doing to us. You have brought misery, destruction and death to my country."

"Yes, I know, it has been terrible for you," said Peter. "But we are trying to help you build things again. And we have suffered too. My best friend Luke lost both his legs to an I.E.D. He almost killed himself afterwards."

"War," said Marriam. "I hate war! Why cannot men see that war does not solve anything? How can you help people by bringing war to their country? Both sides suffer in any conflict. But this war was your choice, not ours. We did not invite you here, or ask for your help. We were happy in our own world. We hate those who interfere in our affairs, no matter who they are or what their reasons."

"I understand, believe me. But I did not choose this war. Yes, I am an American soldier, and I must do my duty. But I had no choice about coming here. I did what I was told to do – keep Afghanistan from being crushed by the Taliban – and defend my own country from terrorism." He paused again.

"But please," he continued, his tone changing entirely. "This war has nothing to do with what I feel about you. All I ask is to talk with you, to get to know you better. I'm not just a soldier. I'm a human being."

"You may want to know me," said Marriam, "but I do not want to know you. I want nothing to do with Americans. Americans killed my brother! Leave now, or I will call security."

"Wait," said Peter. "Please wait. He cast about desperately for some way to reach out to her. "I will go in a second, I swear. But first, give me your email address. That's all I ask. Let me write to you. You don't have to answer. You don't even have to read what I say."

It was a defining moment, Peter knew. She would walk out of the door, he was certain. She would make sure he was never again allowed in the school.

But instead, she hesitated, staring at him across the room.

"Please," Peter said. "I won't come here again. I won't bother you." He sounded desperate, a man pleading for a final chance. Against her better judgment, she felt sorry for him. If she gave him her email, perhaps he would go away.

"All right," she said softly. "I will give you the address. But do not bother to write. I will never read your emails."

"That's okay," said Peter. "It's up to you." Relief flooded through him. The door was not closed after all. She pulled a pen from her notebook, tore out a page and began to write.

"I must be mad," she said, handing it to him.

"Thank you," he said. "Thank you. You don't know how much this means to me." Suddenly, he was grinning, his face young and strong and happy. He looked like an entirely different person.

How tall he is, thought Marriam. For the first time, she registered his intense blue eyes, his square jaw, and the pale gold of his hair, cut short, military style. *How strange,* she thought. *He is very handsome. And very American.*

"Look out for my emails," said Peter, "You'll see them soon."

What a stupid thing to do, she scolded herself, starting down the hall. *But it's done. I will not think about it. He can send all the emails he wants. I will not read them.* She inhaled deeply. To her surprise, she had been holding her breath.

Peter put his helmet on and watched her walk away.

Chapter Ten

☙

As the one who had invited Shahnawaz to lunch, Claire was determined to impress him. Leaving for work that morning, she chose a pale peach dress scattered with flowers, light make up and rose lipstick. When she examined her reflection in the mirror, she found herself smiling. At work, the minutes dragged. She watched the numbers change on her screen. She had already gathered her things together. As she was about to go, Cathy appeared, went over a checklist, and insisted on seeing a spreadsheet Claire had been working on. Then, she was late. She flew out through the door.

Shahnawaz reached the restaurant ten minutes early, at 12:50, and chose a table with a view of the street. He could feel his heart beating. He was astonished at the turmoil of his emotions. He tried to read the menu, but was so hungry for a glimpse of Claire that he couldn't keep his eyes off the window.

This is ridiculous, he thought. *I'm like a schoolboy. It must be the years without a woman's attention. I just need to see her a few times – then everything will be easy.*

Still, the minutes ticked by slowly. Again and again, he checked his watch. At ten minutes past one, there was still no sign of her.

Maybe she changed her mind, he thought. *Maybe she's not coming.*

But then, there she was, pushing a lock of hair from her face and hurrying towards the door. He felt the blood rise to his cheeks and stared hard at the menu, as if searching for a secret. He didn't want to appear too eager. It seemed inappropriate, embarrassing.

It took Claire a few seconds to find Shahnawaz at the far end of the restaurant, seated at a table by the window, concentrating on the menu. As she walked towards him, she felt her smile getting wider and wider. She stopped a few feet away and waited for him to notice her. He looked up abruptly, and for a moment she froze, startled by the desire in his eyes. Then he smiled, like the sun coming out from a dark cloud, and the intensity dissipated. The whole world seemed a sparkling brightness.

What is happening to me? she thought, terrified. Her smile faded. *It will never work out. And what about Peter? Nothing productive will come of this relationship.*

"Hello, Claire," said Shahnawaz, rising to greet her.

"Hello," she replied, stepping a little closer. She loved hearing him say her name.

"It's so good to see you," he said, raising an eyebrow. "I was worried you might not be coming." He pulled her chair out a little and she sat down.

"Oh dear, I'm late. I'm so sorry to keep you waiting."

"No, no, it's fine. Lunchtime is always difficult. I wasn't going anywhere. I would have waited – at least for another ten minutes." He smiled to show it was a joke. It was good to be with Claire, he realized. He was liking her more and more. Still, he was not sure how to start talking to her.

"So how is your work going?" he said, making conversation.

Claire sighed. "It's okay, I guess. Not so interesting most of the time." She looked directly at him. "As I think I already told you."

Then she smiled. "I haven't forgotten your offer."

"I am glad to hear it. I was not just being polite. I could certainly find a position for you."

"Thank you," said Claire. "I really appreciate that. But honestly, I'm not really sure it's a good idea." Shahnawaz didn't ask why. He was not sure he wanted to know the answer.

The waiter saved him. They ordered their food. To his relief, Claire changed the subject.

"Tell me about yourself," she said. "I don't know anything about you. Where do you live? What do you like? What don't you like? I'd love to know." In fact, she wanted to know everything about this handsome Afghan.

Shahnawaz was surprised at the question, and surprised at himself for attempting to answer. He was seldom in a situation where such conversations came up. And when they did, he usually avoided them.

"I am just an ordinary Afghan immigrant. I came to America looking for some peace and a better life. It is, after all, the land of opportunity, is it not?"

"I hope so," said Claire, feeling emboldened. She determined to find out as much as she could. "Do you have family here? Do you live with someone?"

Shahnawaz hesitated. The question brought too many things to mind.

"No," he said briefly. "I am alone." Then he was silent.

"I'm sorry," said Claire. "I didn't mean to pry."

She was put off by his abrupt answer, Shahnawaz realized – though that was the last thing he wanted. She knew nothing about his past, of course. Her questions were signs of interest. It was rude to push them away.

"No, no. My apologies. I did not mean to reply in such a manner. But questions bring up memories, and memories are painful. I find it best not to think about them too much."

"I'm a good listener," Claire said. "Besides, it's easier to deal with pain if you share it with someone." She paused. "But that's hard to do. I'm not always great at it myself."

"You may well be right about sharing things," said Shahnawaz. He looked in her eyes and gave a sad smile. "Perhaps next time we see each other. But right now, I'm afraid, I do not know you that well."

"Of course," said Claire, heartened by his assumption that there would be a next time. "I don't want to make you uncomfortable. But I'm ready to tell you about me, if you're interested. That's an offer I don't make to everyone."

Shahnawaz was happy to shift the focus to Claire. Besides, he wanted to know.

"Go ahead," he said with a smile of relief. "Tell me everything."

"Well," said Claire, settling into a story-telling mode. "I was an only child. My father was a professor at Boston University, so I grew up in Boston. I loved it – especially the Public Gardens, with the Swan Boats and the duckling statues. And there was wonderful ice cream too." Shahnawaz was enchanted by the classic story of the mother duck who led her line of ducklings through the streets of Boston. As she felt him relax, Claire found it easier and easier to talk. She started telling him about darker things too.

"The truth is, my parents never got along well with each other. They fought a lot. It was loud, and they didn't seem to notice me. In my room at night, even with the door closed, I could hear them." She stopped and stirred her coffee, concentrating on the liquid swirling in the cup. "It was bad. I didn't know who to blame. I loved them both. But I hated them for doing this to me."

"I am sorry to hear this," said Shahnawaz. "It must have been very difficult." He couldn't imagine how anyone could hurt this lovely woman.

"Then, when I was nine, my father got a teaching offer from Oxford University. It was a once-in-a-lifetime offer, he said, a great opportunity. But my mother didn't want to live in England. She asked him to turn it down. And he said no. She told him that she would not go with him – that she wanted a divorce." She paused. "So they got divorced, and he left, and that was that."

"And was it better then?"

She looked up at Shahnawaz and gave a wry smile. "Not really. Better for her maybe. A few years later, she remarried and we moved to Long Island. I have two step brothers and a step sister now."

"At least you had a family," said Shahnawaz, thinking how much he missed his own. "Did you come to care for your stepfather?" He was surprising himself by asking such personal questions.

"No," Claire said sadly, though thinking of him often made her angry. "I never liked him. I sort of lost my Mom too. She wanted to be happy, but I reminded her of her failed marriage, I think. Maybe she still loved my Dad a little too."

"I am sorry that it was hard for you growing up," Shahnawaz said with feeling. He remembered his childhood as a joyful time.

"I left my parents' house as soon as possible," she went on. "I told you that I saw them often. That's not really true." She looked at Shahnawaz, but he didn't seem annoyed.

"Please go on," he said. "I want to hear, I really do."

It was a relief to hear him say it. "After college," she continued, "I stayed in New York and took a job with a family friend. I got the job I have now a couple of years ago. Not my dream job, but it's okay." She paused as if thinking to herself. "It's very important to me to manage on my own." To her surprise, she felt her eyes brimming with tears. She had opened old wounds that had been stitched with difficulty.

Shahnawaz reached across the table and covered her hand gently with his own. Then he offered her an immaculately folded handkerchief from his breast pocket. She smiled and dabbed at her eyes, determined not to smudge her make up.

"I am very sorry to learn that you had such a hard time with your parents," he said with feeling. "You did not have to tell me about your past."

Claire smiled at him. "Yes I did," she said. "I wanted to. I am okay now. Really. I don't know why I started crying. It's something I almost never do."

The conversation was lighter after that. And easier for both of them. Their lunch came, and they discussed the restaurant and agreed on the excellence of new American cuisine. She was glad that Shahnawaz liked the place.

"Now," said Shahnawaz, as if about to make an announcement, "I believe it is time for you to taste my country's food. There's an excellent Afghan restaurant not far from where you live. Would you care to join me for dinner this Saturday?"

"I'd love to," said Claire, grinning from ear to ear. She would have gone anywhere with him.

"Then that is settled," said Shahwanaz, delighted to have arranged another meeting before she slipped away again. "I will be at your place at seven."

"Perfect. I will be there too."

They lingered over dessert and coffee. Then Shahnawaz looked at his watch.

"Oh dear," he said, "you must be late getting back to your office. You will anger the evil Ms. Hardwick again. We cannot let that happen."

"No worries. I am free – I arranged to take the rest of the day off!"

Shahnawaz's eyes sparkled. "Then, may I suggest we spend some time together? Perhaps you would guide me through some New York attractions."

"I think I could do that." She was grinning from ear to ear.

* * *

The subway was the fastest way to the bottom of the island. They strolled through Battery Park, pink petals beneath their feet. The cherry trees were in bloom.

"Have you been to The Statue of Liberty?" asked Claire.

"No. I have never found time for sightseeing, I'm afraid."

"Then you have seen nothing. That will be our first stop. We can get the ferry just a few blocks from here."

"Whatever you say. I will follow you." He was delighted that she was taking her role so seriously.

They reached Battery Park and bought their tickets inside Castle Clinton's imposing sandstone walls.

"This was actually the first place immigrants came through," said Claire. "It was built about 1810."

The ferry ride to Ellis Island was exhilarating. They went out on the open deck, the wind whipping their hair. Shahnawaz took Claire's hand. Soon, the colossal figure of Liberty was towering over them, raising her torch triumphantly above New York Harbor.

"She's magnificent, isn't she?" said Claire. "She was a gift to America from France in 1886. There's a poem inscribed on the base. It's old fashioned and kind of patronizing, but the final lines are so beautiful – *Give me your tired, your poor/ Your huddled masses yearning to breathe free,/ The wretched refuse of your teeming shore./ Send these, the homeless, tempest-tossed to me,/ I lift my lamp beside the golden door!*"

"How do you know all this?" asked Shahnawaz, astonished.

"I don't know. When I first moved here, I wanted to learn all about the city. I couldn't get enough."

They spent the rest of the day like happy tourists, examining the displays and photos in the Immigration Museum, riding up inside the statue and marveling how it was built over a century ago. Then they just wandered around the island, holding hands, laughing, and gazing at the water.

"I have been in New York for years now," said Shahnawaz, crunching the last of an ice cream cone. "But I have never seen places like this. It seems I was missing a lot."

"You never did any sightseeing?"

"When I came to the United States, I was a refugee. And,

to be truthful, I was deeply depressed. I wanted only to forget my miserable past and secure myself a future. And for that, I worked fifteen hours a day. And I managed to earn a lot of money. That, at least, I accomplished."

"And what makes you so interested in New York now?"

"I must admit, it is only because of you. Because of you, I no longer feel so chained to the past. I am not exactly free, mind you. But you've helped me remember that there is more to life than just working and brooding."

Claire watched a small boat speed across the harbor. It bobbed violently as it crossed the wake of a ferry, then recovered itself and went on. Was it wise to get involved with this handsome foreigner, this complicated guarded man who made her so happy? And what about Peter? She didn't know what she felt about him anymore.

"Claire?" Shahnawaz said, breaking her reverie. "I have a suggestion. If you would be my guide again, we could do some more sightseeing on Saturday. I could come to your place about noon. We could have a bite, do our tour, and finish with dinner at my Afghan restaurant."

"What a great idea. There are so many places to show you – Central Park, the Empire State Building, the zoo. We could walk across the Brooklyn Bridge sometime, if it's a nice day. And there are all the museums too!"

"This Saturday, however," said Shahnawaz, laughing, "we will have to choose."

"But there's one thing I should tell you," she added. Shahnawaz looked concerned.

"I absolutely have to change before dinner."

The corners of his eyes wrinkled as he smiled. "I'm sure I will be happy with what you are already wearing. But if you like, I will bring you back to your apartment for whatever you need to do."

They were excited as two teenagers planning an adventure. Then Shahnawaz glanced at his watch. "It's late," he said. "I must buy you dinner."

"Oh Shahnawaz, I don't think I can manage it. We had such a big lunch."

"I agree. How about some street food?"

He took her home in a taxi and walked her upstairs, waiting while she opened the door.

"Last time we were here," he said, "there were flowers."

Claire remembered only too well. The flowers – and, most clearly, the kiss that came later. She yearned for him to kiss her again.

Instead, he put his hands on her shoulders and kissed her forehead.

"OK, I'll see you Saturday," he said.

"Yes," she said. "You definitely will." She felt like an alcoholic with a glass of whiskey held before her, then poured away. She went into the apartment and watched through the peephole while he waited for the elevator. She could not see that he was trembling all over.

In fact, Shahnawaz was remembering the last time in her apartment too – every second of it. He wanted to kiss her again, to feel the softness of her mouth, to melt into her until time vanished. But he remembered the shame he had felt afterwards too. He was determined not to rush things, for either of them. It was their first date, after all, and he was acutely aware of being a foreigner and an Afghan. She was an American. They must learn to trust each other. He pushed that last encounter from his mind and concentrated on Saturday.

As the elevator closed, Claire turned and looked at herself in the mirror on the hall door. Her cheeks were flushed and her eyes sparkling. Her reflection smiled back at her.

Why am I so happy? she wondered. *This is ridiculous. It's almost like falling in love.*

* * *

In the following days, all Claire could think of was Shahnawaz. But Peter kept coming to mind too. Each time he did, a wave of guilt washed over her. Her friends assumed that Peter's posting in Afghanistan was the only reason they had not announced their engagement. At first, she had agreed with them. But the more she thought about their time together over Christmas, the more she realized that their relationship was on truly shaky ground. Peter had left with nothing resolved between them. They had not even spent that much time together.

Maybe, she thought, *I do not love him anymore.* The idea of love immediately brought Shahnawaz to mind. *Maybe,* she thought, *I never did truly love him.*

She was afraid to share these thoughts with Peter. Still, he was so far away, and in such danger. How could she let him down? She wanted to be fair. She determined to write more about Shahnawaz, their friendship, and the closeness that was developing between them. She hoped Peter would begin to understand.

This decision lifted a weight from her mind, and she sat down and wrote Peter a joyful email which included not only gossip about friends, and an account of the beauties of spring in the city, but a lengthy description of her day with Shahnawaz at the Statue of Liberty, and how much she had enjoyed it. She mentioned that she was seeing him again on Saturday.

At the end, she screwed up her courage and wrote:

I miss you, of course, but at Christmas, we weren't as close as we used to be. We've taken things for granted for a long time. Maybe we should back off a little. Maybe we should take a break.

Then, she realized, she had nothing more to say, and she ended the email rather abruptly. She pressed "send", put her head back, closed her eyes, and let her thoughts drift into visions of Saturday and another glorious day with Shahnawaz – no longer an Afghan or a stranger, but a man who needed love.

Chapter Eleven

⚜

Peter thought of nothing but Marriam – her beautiful face, her musical voice, her green eyes. It was almost impossible for him to concentrate on work. He snapped at his men. At his computer, words and figures blurred, and her face appeared before him; if he was walking, he felt her presence at his side. When he looked, of course, there was no one – yet he felt her absence acutely.

This is not normal, he thought. *I'm going crazy. I said I would email her, and I must. I have to tell her that I love her.*

The next day, he tried to express his feelings in an email. But though emotions welled up instantly, words were not so easy. He had cared deeply about Claire, believed he loved her. But he had never felt anything like this before. Finally, he managed to write a few truthful lines to Marriam. His heart almost stopped as he pressed the "send" button.

He tried in vain not to be anxious as he awaited a reply. For a few days, he managed to hold back his disappointment, then forced himself to wait a few days more before sending another imploring email. No answer.

He began to feel unhinged. He imagined a hundred irrational scenarios in which he found ways to catch Marriam's attention – in one, he saw himself standing at the gates of the school playing his guitar and singing love songs until she came out smiling, arms outstretched to comfort him. He jokingly threatened to do this in an email. Still, no answer.

His work started to suffer. His superior officer called him into his office.

"Captain Jenkins," said Major Richards, seated behind his desk. A map of Afghanistan hung on the wall behind him, divided into zones by colors. "You have always been an excellent soldier. But I've been hearing complaints lately. You were late to maneuvers twice, and you said nothing at all at the last staff meeting. Even the Colonel noticed. Is something the matter?"

"Nothing, sir." He could hardly say he was in love with an Afghan woman.

"Look, Jenkins, this is not a training exercise; it's a war zone. Discipline is at the heart of what we do here. How can we expect the Afghans to learn from us if we don't set them an example? How can we expect them to keep order on their own? You will lose the confidence of your men too. Sloppiness and negligence lead to casualties." His voice was rising. "I will not tolerate it."

Peter said nothing.

"Do you understand me, Captain?" He was shouting now.

"Yes, sir."

"Make sure you do," continued the Major, his voice lower, but its intensity undiminished. "If anything happens – if a single soldier is harmed because of your carelessness, I will hold you personally responsible."

"Yes, sir."

"So stop being an idiot and start being an officer. Now get out. I don't want to see you here again."

"Yes, sir. Absolutely, sir." Peter saluted briskly, turned on his heel and marched back to his office.

The Major's words were a reality check. *It's time to stop this day dreaming*, he thought. *It's useless – and unforgivable. The men rely on me. We depend on each other. I can't risk their lives like some stupid kid in love.*

His work improved. The Major called him in to commend him.

Still, Marriam was always on his mind.

* * *

Peter's men continued their patrols around the school. Each time he drove by, it was a physical effort not to go in and ask for Marriam, or tell his driver to stop, so he could wait for her to appear.

One afternoon, after the students had left, he saw a black SUV pull up in front of the gate. The driver got out, walked around, and opened the rear door. As he did, the gate opened, and there she was, unmistakable – tall and graceful and confident. A strand of hair had escaped from her *hijab*. He felt weak with love.

His driver Jones had had a terrible cold that morning, and Peter had told him to stay on base, glad for an excuse to be on his own. Now that decision was paying off. He followed the black car outside the city, through more and more problematic areas, thinking only, *Marriam is inside. I must find where she is going.*

The car stopped in front of a large house with high walls

and a watchtower. Two men opened the massive metal gates, and the car disappeared inside.

So this is where she lives. Peter thought. He looked long and hard, memorizing every detail he could see. Finally, he drove back to the base, feeling happier than he had for a long time, as if he had brought a part of Marriam back with him.

* * *

About an hour after his return, Major Richards appeared at his office door.

"Were you driving the jeep, Captain?"

"Yes, sir."

"No doubt you are aware that it's against regulations to drive alone. This is not some high school excursion. Beyond the Green Zone, you must have someone with you. Your safety depends on it. And the men's safety too."

"My driver was in a bad way this morning, sir."

"The directive is simple, Captain – do not go beyond the Zone by yourself. That is an order. Understood?"

"Yes, sir. It won't happen again, sir."

Peter knew that the Major was right. It was not his place to question orders. Still, his judgment was clouded, and he did not regret for an instant what he had done. Following Marriam trumped dangers and directives. It was a top priority.

Later the same day, he sent Marriam a last, desperate email. If he did not hear from her, he wrote, he would come to her house and stand outside until someone saw him and brought him in.

He did not expect a reply. But this time, he got one.

* * *

Marriam was scanning her email when she saw Peter's message. There had been so many. Usually, she deleted them with hardly a second thought. But this subject line scared her – *I know where you live* – and she clicked it open. The message itself sounded extreme, unhinged, passionate. *Surely*, she thought, *this must be an empty bluff.* But what if it wasn't? Ignoring his messages had had no effect, but maybe a direct reply would put him off. Maybe he would listen to reason. She wrote....

  Dear Captain Jenkins,
  Last time we met, I told you that I would not read your emails, and up to now, I have not read a single one. But your subject line compelled me to open this. What you propose is dangerous and inappropriate, and I pray that you are not seriously considering it. I implore you, for your own sake and for mine too, stay away. If you came to my home, you would put us both in terrible danger. My people see you as an enemy. Americans killed my brother. This is not a joke.

  Sincerely,
  Marriam

When Peter saw Marriam's email in his inbox, relief flooded through him. His joy at her response was a testament to his state of mind. He read her words again and again, choosing to see them as a golden opportunity, a miraculously open door. *Now at least she is listening,* he reasoned, and redoubled his efforts to establish a connection, emailing her every day, as if she were expecting to hear from him.

The emails told her how often he thought of her, but they were calmer now, chatty, full of everyday thoughts and feelings. He told her of his life in America, his wonderful friends and family, regaled her with tales of his childhood, his love of school, his first driving lesson, as if she were dying to know. He recounted funny stories, pranks he played with friends, the time he went surfing and got stung by a jellyfish. He did his best to describe the ocean to her. He ended each email the same way: "*I need to see you and talk to you, Marriam. I love you.*"

With each email, Peter felt closer to her. He told her about Claire, and how he they had been practically engaged. But, he went on, his feelings for Marriam had eclipsed all others.

Not long after that, he received an email from Claire herself devoted mostly to Shahnawaz, but he didn't mind at all. He was deeply relieved to discover that she too had been having doubts and replied immediately, explaining that though he cared deeply for her, he too felt that they had drifted apart. He suggested that they rethink their relationship.

Marriam didn't reply to Peter's emails, but she began reading them. Clicking on that single message was like opening a door through which she could never return. As she read them, her anger about her brother's death receded. He had been many years older, and she had hardly known him. And Peter himself had not been responsible.

She found herself fascinated as Peter introduced her to an entirely new world. Before she realized it, he was no longer just a handsome American soldier with an irrational passion for her – he was becoming someone she felt she knew. She even went back and read his earlier messages. For some reason she had not understood herself, she had never deleted them.

When she read about Claire, Marriam smiled with relief. But not for the reasons that Peter had intended. If he was so easily distracted from someone he had practically been engaged to, she reasoned, surely he would soon forget her too.

But that did not happen, and after a while, the urgency in the emails resurfaced. They became passionate and imploring, as if he could not bear being separated from this woman he hardly knew.

He wrote:

Claire and I have reached an understanding. I have no further moral obligation to her, except as an old friend. She herself has established another relationship. There is no question in my mind as to what I must do: I am determined to come to your house and ask your father for your hand in marriage.

This message shocked Marriam. It didn't sound like a bluff. Once more, she felt compelled to reply:

Please, Peter, she wrote – formality did not seem appropriate any more – *Do not even think of coming to my house. My father's people would surely kill you. An American soldier cannot marry an Afghan woman. Even in peace time it is not possible for me to marry outside my religion.*

Peter found a way to interpret even this message as encouraging. She was reading his emails; he had engaged her attention; she was becoming involved. The process was slow, but inevitable, he felt, for he would never give up. Sooner or later, she would fall in love with him.

Chapter Twelve

☙

On Saturday, Shahnawaz arrived at Claire's door at 10 am precisely.

Claire had been ready for some time. She was sitting on the edge of the couch, a bit anxious. *What if the phone rings,* she thought, *and he says he cannot come.*

When the bell rang, she sprang to her feet smiling, and rushed to the door. There stood Shahnawaz, as handsome as ever. She opened the door wide and gave an enormous smile.

Shahnawaz could not help smiling too. He felt like a small boy who had just opened a box full of toys.

"Come in, come in," she said, stepping back only slightly.

"Hello Claire," he said in his deep, rich voice. "I am so glad to see you."

"Me too."

He moved towards her, until only a few inches separated them. She stood her ground. He bent over, trying to assess her reaction. Claire turned her face up to him, and looked into his eyes, waiting to see what he would do.

Shahnawaz touched his lips to hers, tentatively at first,

unsure how she might respond. But the response was instantaneous. She kissed him back with such passion that it took his breath away.

Last time was real, he thought, *she felt it too.* And his whole being flooded with joy.

His kiss became bolder and more demanding. Claire parted her lips and his tongue slipped between them. Then suddenly, their mouths were open, hungry, merging with each other. Time and thought disappeared; all that existed was this moment. The world shrank to encompass only the two of them, but together, their passion filled the universe.

Shahnawaz wrapped Claire in his arms and she came willingly. He lifted his head for a moment to look at her, then started kissing her everywhere – her eyelids, her cheeks – she put her head back, exposing her throat to him, and he lingered at the softness beneath her jaw. He ran his tongue around the delicate geometry of her ear, then kissed his way down her neck to the hollow at the base of her collarbone. Her body responded to his in perfect harmony. But he did not stop there, he could not – he ran his tongue down toward the softness of her breasts, and she shuddered with passion.

Shahnawaz felt her shudder in every atom of his being – and it brought him to his senses. He stepped back, opened his eyes and took a deep breath, his hands on her shoulders, as if enforcing a distance between them.

She opened her eyes wide and gave him a look of utter bewilderment.

"I am so sorry," he said, his voice soft and husky, as though it were difficult to speak. "I got carried away – again. I don't know what is the matter with me. I should not have done that."

Claire searched his handsome face for a clue as to what she had done to provoke this.

"No, no…. it was okay. Really." She had no idea what to say. She had never seen a man act this way before.

"No. It was not okay. You do not understand. I am so sorry."

"Please, Shahnawaz, sit down and talk to me." Her voice was trembling, her body still humming with passion.

"Dammit," he murmured, running his fingers through his hair, and looked around for a chair to sit on.

Claire felt hollow, a cool whiteness fogging the warm joy she had felt only a few moments earlier. *This is so weird*, she thought, *as if he is ashamed of kissing me.*

"There is nothing to apologize for, Shahnawaz. Really. I am so confused. Are we going out or not?"

"Yes, Claire, yes. Of course we are going out. Only… I was not ready for what just happened." He rubbed his eyes with the heels of his hands, trying to bring himself down to earth again, to understand how he could have been so quickly swept away.

"What do you mean?" said Claire. "Don't you find me attractive?"

"Oh God, Claire. Do I find you attractive? What do you think? I cannot keep myself from touching you. Look, Claire, please try to understand. I am a Muslim. We are not allowed to touch women who are strangers to us."

"Strangers, Shahnawaz? I am a friend – at least I hoped so."

"Yes, yes, of course – a good friend, a dear friend, and I like you enormously. But to kiss you that way is to invade your sanctity. It is not allowed in my religion."

"Wait, Shahnawaz, what are you saying?" The frustration was making her irritated now. "I didn't feel invaded. I encouraged you. Is faith blocking your feelings? Can it destroy our connection?"

"No! No! Please try to understand. I want us to be friends, more than anything in the world. But I must not let my feelings get the better of me. From now on, I will do my best not to touch you in an inappropriate way. Let us put this incident aside. Let us return to the day we planned."

"All right," said Claire. "If that's what you need to do."

The joy of their encounter had been replaced by uncertainty and confusion. It had felt so right; she had been sure he felt it too. If not, what was he feeling? She loved this sad Afghan, and wanted him to love her; and yet, again and again, he set up barriers between them. She determined to collect herself and move forward. It was the only thing she could think to do.

"How about some tea?" she said, eager to find a practical distraction. "And we can talk about where to go from here – our day, I mean. What we're going to do."

"Yes, please," said Shahnawaz, hugely relieved to change the subject.

She made tea, and they planned their afternoon: another real tourist moment – the view from Rockefeller Center – then a stroll down 5th Avenue to Central Park, and perhaps a stop at the Metropolitan Museum. They ate sandwiches at a coffee shop and walked and walked. They never made it to the Met – they rode the carousel instead, like happy children. In fact, it was a lovely day.

* * *

At the end of the afternoon, Shahnawaz brought Claire back to her apartment as he had promised. He sat in the living room with a magazine, while she went into her bedroom to change. She opened her closet and stared at the bright row of dresses hanging in it. It was hard to choose one, but not for the usual reasons. She thought back to the moment when Shahnawaz had pushed her away, and barely managed to keep herself from bursting into tears.

I am little more than a stranger to him, she thought, *just a casual friend. And he wants to keep it that way.*

She felt drained of energy. What was the point of dressing up for Shahnawaz anyway? She chose the first dress that came to hand. Still, she looked very pretty.

They had dinner at an Afghan restaurant in The Village. The setting was lovely, the waiters charming. But Shahnawaz was acutely aware of Claire's change of mood. The Claire he had kissed had disappeared; even the vivacious woman he had spent the afternoon with seemed gone, replaced by someone remote, as if there were a pane of glass between them. He felt desperate to ease the tension. But he had no idea how. *Maybe she just needs a little space*, he thought. He wanted to respect her privacy. Still, he could not stop himself from asking.

"What is the matter, Claire? You seem so quiet."

"Nothing."

"Is it what happened earlier today? Before we went out?"

She looked up at him sadly.

"Look, Claire. Perhaps I did not explain myself properly. I need you to understand. The way you live here in New York is very different from the way I was raised in Afghanistan. From the time I was born, I was brought up with strict Islamic rules. Men and women are separated from each other. There are schools for boys, and schools for girls. There, we learn not only how to read and write, but how to behave. When a girl grows up, she must wear a *hijab*, covering her clothes and body. Only her face is visible outside her family. America has affected me in many ways. I am not the same as when I arrived so many years ago. But I am still a Muslim at heart. Please forgive me if I have hurt your feelings. I would never do so on purpose."

Claire felt ashamed of her anger.

"Thank you, Shahnawaz, for telling me all this. I've never kissed someone and had them turn away from me before. It's hard not to think that maybe you don't really like me. I understand more now – at least, I'm beginning to."

"So we are friends again?" he asked. Finally, she was smiling.

"Of course we are." She reached out for his hand, and with the touch, she could feel the tension drifting away. They could enjoy their meal.

The food was scrumptious, just as he had promised. They ordered naan and kebabs and lamb biryani, followed by a delicate, creamy dessert, sweet with honey and scented with rosewater, and refreshing green tea. Shahnawaz told her about Afghan traditions; they talked about everything.

Hours later, Shahnawaz brought Claire back to her apartment. The tension rose as she opened the door with her key.

"Thank you for a really lovely evening," she said, turning slightly to looking at him. She started to step through the door, but Shahnawaz put his hand on her shoulder.

"Am I forgiven?" he asked, his voice soft and serious.

"There is nothing to forgive." She smiled and turned to face him.

"In that case......" He held her face in his hands and kissed her forehead. Then he gazed into her eyes and saw them misty with desire. Her lips were moist, already parted, soft as rose petals. Helpless to resist, he bent forward and kissed her lightly, just a thank you kiss. But Claire's response was immediate, as if the force of passion he was struggling to rein in was drawing her to him. Resolutions were all very well, but Shahnawaz was no saint. He kissed her back with equal passion. Again, the extraordinary phenomenon of forgetting everything but the sensation of the moment. Again, time standing still.

He hardly noticed the vibration, but the ring of his cell phone could not be ignored, insistent, cruel, louder and louder. He stepped back and fumbled in his pocket.

"What the hell!" he muttered. Claire stood back, trembling. He glanced at the screen. It was his manager. The spell was broken.

Claire crossed her arms and hugged herself, trying to calm her breathing, doing her best to grapple with the passion she felt whenever this man touched her. People talked about chemistry – this was more like a nuclear reaction. She waited for Shahnawaz to finish the call.

He put the phone in his pocket and looked at her sheepishly. The look was so gentle and humble she had to smile.

"Just a few hours ago, I promised to keep my hands off you, but I have failed utterly. There are no more apologies in me. I surrender."

Claire laughed. "About time." She shook her finger at him. "You are shameless indeed and not to be forgiven." Her heart was singing with joy.

"So what happens now?" He looked deeply concerned.

"I don't have the slightest idea," she said, shrugging her shoulders. "I've never dealt with anything like this before. All I know is that I value my friendship with you more than anything on earth. Can we manage this relationship as friends? Do you think it's a good idea?" She looked up at him hopefully, still unsure of his response.

"Oh! It is a great idea. The best idea I have ever heard." His smile was warm as the sun.

"We will just have to figure it out together."

"You have my complete cooperation. So, when shall we see each other again?"

"We can plan something for next week, if you can find time for me. You are a very busy man, I know," she added, tilting her head flirtatiously.

"Of course I will find time for you. You are irresistible." He took a step back, holding her hands, and looked at her. "Goodbye now, Claire. I will not come in. Right now, I cannot trust myself. But I will see you very soon."

He gave her hands a squeeze, turned quickly, and walked down the corridor.

Chapter Thirteen

⋈

Peter's passion for Marriam grew and grew. He thought of her every waking moment. Only sleep brought a few hours' relief. He wrote her email after email, but after her second stern note of warning, there was no reply.

He thought more and more about going to her house, meeting her father, and declaring his love. The danger seemed nothing compared to the strength of his desire to see Marriam.

Finally, he could bear it no longer. He knew that he could not just go and knock on the door – but he found hope in the deep-seated Afghan traditions of honor and hospitality. The Afghans hated Al Qaeda – yet when Osama Bin Laden chose their country as a refuge, they had not forced him to leave. If Peter presented himself, perhaps he would be invited in. It was a risk worth taking.

This time, he knew, he had to take his driver. Perhaps it was for the best. If things did not go well, he would be waiting – ready to drive off quickly, or carry news of disaster back home. But Jones had something to say himself.

"That area is beyond our jurisdiction, sir. We have to take an escort. Colonel's orders."

"I know, I know," Peter answered, annoyed.

"I could arrange an armored vehicle to accompany us."

"All right." It was no longer a question of if, but how. "Do whatever you need to."

The vehicles left the compound together at 1300 hours, passed uneventfully through the Green Zone, then continued beyond, driving slowly beyond the city. Peter insisted the jeep take the lead. There was little traffic.

A truck appeared from a side road and pulled ahead of them. A hundred yards later, it stopped suddenly and four Afghans jumped out. The Americans stopped too.

The Afghans approached the jeep, shouting and waving their arms, apparently unarmed. Jones leaned out of the window, then brought his head back in.

"They are asking for help, sir. They say that a man in the truck has had a heart attack."

The radio crackled. It was the armored vehicle, warning them to ignore the civilians.

"You want me to drive around them, sir?"

"No," said Peter. "We're here to help these people. So let's help them."

He swung his legs out of the jeep, and all hell broke loose.

The Afghans were reaching into their garments, drawing weapons, shooting. More poured from the back of the truck. Peter felt something punch into his leg, and automatically dove for the ground. The troops behind him had already opened fire. But the Afghans were shielded by Peter's car.

Peter looked up to see his driver slumped over the wheel, his body riddled with bullets. The wound in his leg burned fiercely. Bullets whizzed around him. He could hear them ricocheting off the escort vehicle. Even before he heard its engine, he knew what would happen. In situations where it was not possible to help, orders were to save remaining lives. A helicopter would come to pick up casualties. The escort vehicle backed, screeched in a tight turn, and drove off.

At some point, Peter felt another punch, in his bicep this time. Everything seemed to be happening in slow motion. As if from a distance, he heard the attackers drive off. He glanced at the ground, then registered that the dark stain spreading across the dirt was his own blood. *I'm dying*, he thought. And then, *Marriam...*

* * *

A few minutes later, a civilian car drew up behind the jeep, pulled around it, and sped past as if nothing had happened. From the other direction, a black SUV approached. It slowed down.

Marriam was inside.

"Stop the car, Wajid," she said to the driver. "People are wounded."

"Miss Marriam," he replied sternly, "Malik Sahib has instructed us to avoid such situations."

"I told you to stop," said Marriam. It was clearly an order.

"As you say, Miss." Marriam's driver stopped the car and got out. He glanced at the aide slumped over the wheel of the jeep, went over to Peter, and felt for the pulse in his neck. Marriam rolled the window down.

"The driver is dead," said Wajid. "This man is living."

"He needs help. Pick him up and put him on the back seat." She got out and sat in the front.

Where to take the wounded American was not in question. People in the area were actively hostile to foreign forces. They drove back to Marriam's house.

At the gate, the driver honked three times – a signal that they were bringing in a casualty. The gate swung open, and the car entered the compound, which was dominated by a big house with an expansive lawn. There was a garden on one side, and, on the other, farther back, an infirmary with a small operating theatre for basic surgery – considered a necessity in these turbulent times for those who could afford it. Government hospitals often provided inferior treatment, and bullet wounds or other questionable injuries provoked difficult, unwanted questions.

The medical staff eased Peter from the car. Marriam did not linger to watch them. She was fed up with war. She had been born when Afghanistan was fighting the Russians; had grown up under the harsh regime of the Taliban; now foreign troops were fighting Afghans once more.

Though she lived a privileged life, she did as much as she could to alleviate the misery of ordinary people. Their plight seemed to worsen no matter who was responsible for the conflict. Why couldn't men use brain power instead of their muscle to resolve their differences? Their solution always seemed unquestioning violence.

Her father was in the dining room, expecting her for lunch. He looked up as she entered.

"*Assalam-o-alaikum*, Agha Jan," she said, using a title of respect and wishing him peace like a dutiful daughter.

"*Wah alaikum*," he replied reflexively. There was a pause. "I hear that you have brought in an injured man.'

"Yes, Agha Jan."

"Who is he?"

"I do not know."

"Then why did you bring him here?" There was irritation in his voice.

"We heard bullets in the distance, Agha Jan, so we slowed down. But then the shooting stopped, and a truck with Taliban drive past us. There had been a fight, but it was over. We saw an American vehicle driving away in the distance. There was still a jeep in the road with a dead man at the wheel. But another man was lying on the street. He was alive. So I told Wajid to get him into the car, and we brought him home."

"But he is our enemy. You knew that. Why would you bring him here?"

"He was bleeding, Agha Jan. If I had left him there, he would surely have died."

"Perhaps. But that is not our business. The Americans take care of their own."

"He may be an American, Agha Jan," said Marriam firmly. "But he is also a human being."

"You are too soft hearted for your own good, my daughter."

As the chief of his tribe, Malik Wajahat-Ullah was universally feared and respected. To answer him back was unthinkable. But Marriam was his favorite, with the courage of her convictions, and she spoke to him candidly, from her heart. He was annoyed at the danger and inconvenience, but inwardly pleased at her courage and passion, which reflected his own.

"All right, all right. We will try to save his life. But as soon as he has the strength, he must go."

"Yes, Agha Jan."

* * *

Later that afternoon, a servant came and told Marriam that she could come and see the wounded American. The man lay unmoving on the farthest of the five beds, covered in bandages, his face turned towards the wall. She walked over quietly and stood by the bedside, wondering about the wisdom of what she had done.

When she saw his face, she drew in her breath and stood still, wide-eyed, her hand to her mouth. The doctor came up beside her.

"Yes, Miss," he said, mistaking her reaction for shock at what she saw. "He has sustained major injuries. In fact, his condition is critical. I have removed the bullets, but he has lost a great deal of blood. He may never awaken. Do you know his name?"

"No," she said softly. "He was unconscious when we found him." That part, at least, was true.

A wave of unexpected grief swept over her. "Please, God," she prayed silently, "don't let him die."

* * *

For the next two days, Marriam visited the infirmary each morning. Peter was young and strong and in peak condition. Slowly, his prognosis improved. Still, he drifted in and out of consciousness, groaning occasionally, unaware of his surroundings.

She could have spoken briefly to the doctor and gone away each time, of course. But instead, she lingered at his bedside, studying his features, the way his body lay on the bed, and his strong, elegant, pale hands, motionless on the sheet. Occasionally she spoke a few words of encouragement to him under her breath, so that no one would hear. She felt that it was crucial for him to live, though she did not question why.

"Please, please do not die," she whispered on the third day. The wish came from her heart.

"I am not going to die," he said, his voice weak and raspy from disuse. His eyes opened.

Marriam took a step back, as if to avoid his gaze. But he was staring at her.

"Marriam?" he said. "Marriam? Where am I? Is it really you?"

She felt protective as a mother, hugely relieved, yet annoyed that he had put himself in harm's way.

"Yes, Peter, it is Marriam. Why did you come here? I told you not to come. It is dangerous outside the Green Zone."

"Where am I?" he asked again. "What are you doing here?"

"You were attacked by Taliban and I found you and brought you here. This is my father's house. You are in our infirmary. There was nowhere else to go."

Peter closed his eyes again, struggling through a haze of pain, trying to remember. He felt the grit of the road beneath his cheek, the taste of dirt, the dark patch spreading beneath him. Blood. The sound of yelling and bullets and screeching tires. The image of Jones slumped over the wheel swam into his mind.

"My men. Where are my men?"

"Some drove away. I'm not sure how many. When I got there, only you were alive, and you were unconscious. I didn't even know who you were. There was a man dead in your jeep. Your attackers left – they must have thought that you were dead too. I told my driver to pick you up, and we brought you here. You cannot stay. The moment you are strong enough, you will be driven to the Green Zone, and our men will leave you there."

"My God," said Peter. "Don't send me away yet. I'm here now. I just got here."

"That is not true. You have been lying here unconscious for over two days. I will have them bring you something to eat."

She turned away from him.

"Don't go," pleaded Peter. "Please don't go. The food can wait."

"I cannot stay," she said firmly. "You must understand."

"Please, Marriam."

"Do not use my name. You are putting our lives in danger. No one here knows that I know you. But they know that you are an American, and they see you as an enemy – the enemy who invaded us without provocation. The enemy who killed my eldest brother!"

"I know, I know," he said weakly, feeling the hopelessness of it all. His body throbbed with pain, and his head was splitting. But more than anything, he wanted Marriam to stay.

"Marriam!" The voice was loud. It came from the doorway.

Marriam froze and glanced over her shoulder. Peter knew immediately that this was her father.

"I will come again," she whispered quickly, and turned to face the door.

"The injured man is awake, Agha Jan," she said in Pashto, sounding cool, efficient and unconcerned. "I will order some soup and bread for him."

She walked past her father without looking back. The older man's eyes rested on Peter with suspicion. Peter moaned and turned away, as if he had not seen him.

* * *

Peter managed to swallow some soup and bread and some hot milk. In spite of his wounds, he felt a glimmer of strength. But his mind, as painful as his body, was becoming clearer too.

Oh God, he thought, *finally, I am in Marriam's house. But I am helpless. These people can do anything they want with me. I was weak and selfish, and Jones is dead because of it. And Marriam is in danger too. What have I done?*

Guilt wrapped itself like a dark shroud around him. He closed his eyes and did his best to think.

* * *

American troops collected the body of Peter's driver, but Peter was nowhere to be found. That was both good news and bad. The Afghans removed their own casualties immediately. According to Islam, bodies of the faithful had to be buried within 24 hours. They left Allied bodies to rot. That meant that Peter had been captured – alive.

Now the Army's job was to locate their missing warrior. But the situation was complex. He might be with any of many Afghan factions, some at relative peace with the Allied troops, some actively hostile, some allied with each other, some blood rivals.

Since the altercation had occurred outside the Green Zone, American troops could not conduct a house to house search. Instead, they activated a network of local Afghans paid as agents and informers. Rahim Khan was their key connection in the area. It might take a few days, he told them, to uncover the truth.

Rahim Khan made some judicious inquiries; the word spread. After only a day, a man claimed to have information on Peter's whereabouts. He demanded a thousand dollars to reveal it. That sounded reasonable to Rahim Khan. He went to the Americans and told them that the information would cost them fifteen hundred US dollars. The difference, he would pocket himself.

The Army had funds for such contingencies – this was small change. The deal was approved. Rahim Khan met with his source in a small Kabul cafe and handed over the cash. So, the Army learned that Captain Peter Jenkins was still alive, in the house of the powerful tribal chief Malik Wajahat-Ullah.

Rahim Khan's next job was negotiating for Peter's release. For this, he received an additional sum. The deal he presented to the Americans was an exchange. Three Taliban fighters had been jailed by the Afghan government, and the Taliban were putting pressure on Malik Wajahat-Ullah to use Peter as a bargaining chip. The tribal leader worked to maintain his relations with the Taliban. These captives must be released before Peter would be handed over.

Marriam listened quietly to all that went on in the house. She heard the servants talking too. The situation worried her deeply. Even with pressure from the Americans, the Afghan government would balk at releasing potentially dangerous prisoners. Peter's life was in grave danger.

Chapter Fourteen

CB

Peter was far from Claire's mind. Her attachment to Shahnawaz grew and grew. Still, she wondered about the Afghan's feelings. They spent a lot of time together, and never ran out of things to talk about. But though Claire told him about her childhood, about her parents and friends, her stepfather and the problems he brought with him, Shahnawaz never offered information about himself. He never shared his dreams or fears, talked about his past or family. He seemed to be in pain – but she had no idea why. Her instincts told her that he cared, but he never professed more than friendship for her.

Finally, she resolved to learn more.

Shahnawaz came to pick her up for a movie. But when he arrived, she was not ready to go. Instead, she invited him in.

"I would love to, Claire, of course. But we should leave, or we'll have to sit way down front."

"It doesn't matter. Please come in. I just got some excellent Ethiopian coffee."

Shahnawaz walked in and glanced around. There was no sign or smell of coffee anywhere.

"Do you trust me, Shahnawaz?" she asked, settling herself on the sofa.

"Trust you?" He smiled. "How can I trust you? You invite me in for coffee – yet I do not see a drop of coffee anywhere."

"No, seriously. Am I a really close friend?"

"Of course," said Shahnawaz, sinking into the big armchair. His brow creased with concern. "Why do you ask?"

"I think that you still have reservations about me."

He looked at her hard. "No," he said slowly, with great sincerity. "That is not at all true."

"You say you want to know about me – and I tell you about my childhood, my parents, my past all the time. But after all our time together, you never talk about your family and what happened before you came to the States. Once, you told me that you didn't know me well enough yet to share these things with me. Don't you think we should have gotten beyond that now? I love talking to you. But I feel like I'm giving you so much, and you don't want to share yourself with me at all. I really want to know. Surely, it can't be that bad." She leaned towards him.

Shahnawaz sat quietly for a few moments.

"You are right Claire; and there is a reason."

Claire waited, but he did not elaborate.

"What reason? Aren't I important enough to you?"

"Oh no, Claire," he replied, his voice heavy with sorrow. "It's not that at all." Again, he hesitated. "You are such a joyful woman, Claire. You light up the world around you. There has been much darkness in my life. You would not understand."

"Try me, Shahnawaz. I care about you. I want to know."

Shahnawaz smoothed back his hair, turned his face from her, and looked down at the rug. He shook his head. "No."

"Can you tell me why?"

He did not look at her. Again, he said nothing. A terrible thought loomed in her mind.

"Are you some kind of criminal?" She found herself almost whispering. "Or... a terrorist?"

"What?!" He raised his head. The words were a complete surprise. The idea was so absurd he burst out laughing.

Claire looked at him stared hard at him, frowning. "It's not funny."

"No, no," he said, laughing even harder. "It is not a laughing matter at all."

"Stop it," she cried. "Stop it. I hate you." The laughter subsided. But he still looked amused.

"You do? I am sorry, Claire, but a few seconds ago, you said you felt close to me. Now, I have grown horns on my head? You hate me?" He was still smiling.

"Oh, Shahnawaz, of course I don't hate you. But I don't know what to do. Please, don't tease me anymore. Please tell me your story."

The smile faded.

"All right. But tell me, Claire, what if I am a criminal? What if I have done terrible things? Will you still be my friend?"

"I will be your friend," said Claire, "if you have broken every law there is. If you are the worst human being. I will be more than your friend."

"Why?" He asked softly.

"Because...." It was her turn to hesitate now. "Because I.... I love you." *My God*, she thought, *I've said it.*

Shahnawaz was looking at her in a new way now, as if unsure that he had heard her correctly.

"What about Peter, your Captain who is fighting in Afghanistan?"

"Oh, Peter," she said. "Yes, I care about Peter. I have known him for a long time. And I do love him, in a way. But I had no idea what it meant to love somebody until I met you. A few weeks ago, I emailed Peter and told him that that our relationship did not seem right to me anymore. And, it was weird, but he seemed relieved to hear that. He wrote back and suggested that we put off the engagement indefinitely. He said that he cared for me and wished me well, but I had no more obligation him. And I was glad."

"Oh!" Shahnawaz was staring past her now, if looking into another world. He was quiet for a long time.

Claire's heart sank. *Why did I tell him I love him? He doesn't feel that way himself, and he doesn't know what to say. I'm an idiot. I should never have told him.* Her eyes were brimming with tears.

"I'm sorry I said that I love you. I won't say it again."

"Dammit," said Shahnawaz. He paused.

"Claire, Claire," he continued finally. "Do not apologize. I am honored to hear you say these words. But they also make me want to push you away – I am fearful that if I let you closer to me, you will be sucked into my misery. It is an ocean – it will drown our happiness."

"Why Shahnawaz? Please, tell me what has hurt you so."

"My past is a long story, Claire. A story filled with pain. I wish I could erase it and forget everything. Believe me, I have tried. But I cannot."

Claire waited for him to continue, but again, he was silent.

She reached out and put her small white hand on top of his strong dark one.

"I can see that even remembering hurts, and I am so, so sorry. But I am here for you. I will be okay. I am not afraid, and I believe that sharing that pain will make things easier for you."

"So they say," he said. He was gazing over her shoulder now, out of the window, as if looking into the past and gathering the strength to summon it. After a long time he started speaking, slowly, his voice calm and uninflected, as if reciting a story someone had told him. He told her about his mother, his beloved wife, his tiny daughter, all killed in that single rocket attack on the same day.

"I was in the Army, stationed at Mazar-i- Shareef, far from my village. And we were not at war. Yet I was not able to save a single one of them; I was the one who was safe."

He told her of his father, shot down before his eyes as they laid his family in their graves the very next day. And of his broken promise to protect his little brother, Raby, so young and passionate and true.

"I failed Raby too – all that I had left, gone. I could not save them, but I should have saved him. I have no right to be alive. I should be with them in the heavens."

Tears were streaming down Claire's cheeks now. She did not even try to wipe them away. It was as if she didn't notice them. Shahnawaz's pain echoed inside her, she felt herself vibrating like a tuning fork. She rose suddenly, walked over and stood in front of him, her hands on his shoulders.

"Oh, baby," she said. "I am so, so sorry."

Shahnawaz looked up at her and saw his anguish reflected in her eyes.

"Oh, Claire," he said, with a voice like a sigh. He put his arms around her waist and rested his tired head on her, and she wrapped her arms around him protectively and held him to her. She had never felt so full of love.

Shahnawaz took a few deep breaths, as if attempting to control himself. But to no avail. She could feel his body start to tremble and his chest heave, and then he was crying, sobbing, freeing the pain in his heart. It was the first time in his adult life he had cried before a woman.

She said nothing, but let his tears come, and after some time, the sobs subsided, and she felt him relax against her. She stroked his hair and kissed his head. She felt that she could stand and hold him forever.

They stayed that way for what seemed like a long time. Then Shahnawaz moved his hands to her waist, and sat back, helpless, looking up at her. She wiped the tears from his face, then perched on the arm of the chair beside him, still holding his hand.

"I had no idea how much you had lost. I can't imagine what you have been through. It's incredible that you even got through it."

"I told you my story would make you sad." He reached for his handkerchief and wiped her own tears, just as he had done months ago in the restaurant, when he hardly knew her.

"It doesn't matter," she said. "Thank you for letting me share your sadness. Are you sorry you told me?"

He thought for a moment. "No. I don't think so," he said. "Perhaps it was a good thing to do."

He looked up and smiled at her. "Men don't cry, you know. You must think I'm an incredible sissy." He grinned.

"Totally." She grinned back. "You are lucky that I let people see me with you at all."

Shahnawaz looked serious again. He took her arm, raised the inside of her wrist to his lips and kissed it softly.

"Thank you," he said.

"You are very welcome," she replied. "That's what friends are for."

He looked at his watch. "It seems as if we have missed our movie."

"The reviews were mixed anyway. I'm going to go and wash my face now. And then, I believe, I promised you some coffee."

Chapter Fifteen

ೞ

Marriam was determined to help Peter escape as soon as he had the strength, but he was still very weak, barely able to sit up and eat his food. She feared that the Afghan government would refuse her father's demands, and that the Americans might invade the compound at any time to rescue their missing soldier. Her father's people would defend it without hesitation, she knew – some might be injured, even killed, fighting a far superior force. She felt trapped. How could she choose between her tribe, her family and her people – all central to her being – and this helpless, injured man who adored her?

She became preoccupied with formulating a plan, praying that things went smoothly and no one got hurt. She did her best to make sure that no one noticed her interest in this particular patient. Two other men were now occupying beds in the surgery, and each day she visited all of them, stopping to chat and asking how they were doing.

Peter seemed to be getting better. But he was acting differently too.

"How are you feeling?" she asked.

"I am improving, thank you." The answer sounded stiff and formal. Peter's self-reproach had been growing – he was angry with his weakness in giving way to his impulses. He felt responsible for Jones's death, for endangering Marriam. And deeply guilty.

"You look so sad, Peter," said Marriam. "Is it the pain?"

"I got what I deserved," he said bitterly. "I should never have come here. I behaved like some lovesick kid. My driver died because of me. And here I am, a prisoner – and a burden to you."

Marriam scolded him gently. She did not want to hurt him, but she was determined to discourage any lingering feelings he might have for her.

"I do not wish to say, 'I told you so.' But finally, you are agreeing with me. I tried to tell you that you were risking your life – and the lives of others – that declaring love for me was foolish and dangerous."

"Yes, you did," said Peter. He found it hard to look at her. She leaned slightly towards him and lowered her voice.

"Listen to me. The danger is increasing. The Taliban have found out that my father has an American, and they have pressured him to demand the release of their fighters jailed in Kabul in exchange for your freedom. Malik Wajahat-Ullah is powerful, but he must not anger the Taliban, for they have killed many tribal leaders."

"Dammit," murmured Peter. "This is so bad."

"Miss Marriam!" Someone outside was calling her.

"I must leave now," she whispered. "But I will bring you news as soon as I hear it."

A second later, she was gone.

Peter stared at the wall, feeling crushed by the weight of his own actions. It was up to him, he felt, to make amends, to escape before he caused more harm. He resolved to make it happen soon.

The decision strengthened and calmed him. That night, he slept better than he had since he awoke in the compound.

* * *

While Peter lay in the infirmary, Marriam's nights were full of worry. Often, she lay awake, thinking of how complicated her life had become. Even at school, she found her mind drifting from her students to this impossible problem.

She had deep respect for her father, and admired his leadership, courage and pride. She knew that he would never allow her a relationship with Peter, not only an enemy, but a Christian. In spite of all this, she wanted to help this helpless American with his reckless declarations of love. An unsettling thought crept uninvited into her mind. *Maybe I really do care about him after all.*

* * *

Now that Peter was gaining strength, the painkillers were reduced. He was awake and lucid when she came to the surgery. It made her want to spend more time with him.

This time, as she entered, she could see him watching her from the other side of the room. She spent as little time as she could with the other patients. When she sat down at his bedside, he got right to the point.

"Could I ask you something, Marriam?"

"Of course," she said softly, masking a flash of anxiety.

"I need to know what you feel about me."

She felt uncharacteristically vulnerable, as if he were looking right through her. "What... what do you mean?" She was stalling. She knew what he was asking, but the question seemed to open an abyss of danger. She felt she could not reply honestly. But if she pretended not to care, she feared Peter might do something reckless to force her attention.

"Do you even like me?" he persisted.

"Yes, I like you." She could not deny it.

Her answer made Peter bolder. *Now I must remind her of what I told her when we first met. I must say it to her face again, now*, he thought.

"My feelings have not changed. I love you. You know that I love you. But do you love me at all?"

She took a step back, shocked by the directness of this question – and, even more, by how much it moved her.

"No!" she replied, her voice low and urgent. "Not at all. How could I? You are an invader and an enemy." She was surprised at her own intensity.

To her astonishment, Peter did not seem to mind.

"I know. Of course." He paused to weigh his words. "But let me put it this way – do you like me enough to love me someday? To learn to love me in the future?" He smiled up at her adorably, like a child, his eyes bright with hope.

Now I must talk some sense into him, she thought. *I must explain to him directly.*

"Yes, Peter, I do have feelings for you. But loving you is out of the question,"

"I do not believe you." Peter's expression changed to one of desperation. "I need to hope."

"Why can't you understand?" said Marriam, trying not to raise her voice, "I will never betray my tribe, my people, my

country. I cannot forsake my religion. I would rather die."
Peter was astounded by her passion.

"But I love you so much, Marriam. As much as you love
those things and more. I would do anything to make you love
me."

"That is not the issue. I cannot even think of loving you.
Even the idea of loving you is a sin."

Peter struggled to rein his feelings in, hoping to calm her.
Her cheeks were flushed and she was breathing fast. "Shhh,
shhh, Marriam. It's okay. You have said that you like me.
That's enough for now. My love is boundless. I will wait. I
have enough love for both of us."

She closed her eyes for a few seconds and took a deep
breath.

"Right now," she said, "we must not discuss our feelings.
The only thing that is important is that I help you to escape.
My father is negotiating for the Taliban. If their men are not
released immediately, he will not let you go."

"I am forever grateful for your offer of help, Marriam. But
it is too dangerous for you. I will escape on my own. But first,
I must talk to your father."

"My father?" said Marriam, frowning. "You still want to
talk to my father? What will you say to him?" Suddenly, she
was afraid.

"I will tell him that I love you – that I want to marry you.
For that is the truth."

She was stunned – it was as if he had not heard her at all.

"Are you mad? He might kill you. He may kill me too."

"Surely, he would not kill you. I have heard of traditions
of honor, but everyone says he is a fair man. It doesn't make
sense."

"Please try to see things realistically, Peter. Yours is a different world from ours." Now her eyes were filling with tears. "You are in grave danger. To him, you are an enemy – your people killed his eldest son. I brought you here, and you will be treated well. You are our guest. But if you confess your love for me, you will surely die."

"Then I will die for you."

Marriam felt as if her head would burst with frustration. He had to listen to reason. "What rubbish! I beg you, do not speak of your love or say that you wish to marry me. I love life. I am not ready to die. You must believe me – you are putting me in danger too."

Suddenly, Peter felt very tired. Pain pulsed in his wounds.

"Okay, okay," he said, trying to clear his head. Her features seemed to soften as he gazed at her. He did not feel well at all. "Let me think about it."

She opened her mouth suddenly, as if startled, and her eyes widened. A dark hand was resting on her shoulder. Malik Wajahat-Ullah was standing behind her.

"What are you doing here, daughter?" He spoke in Pashto, his voice deep with fury. Peter could not understand them. "I told you not to come to the surgery."

"Yes, Baba," she replied, addressing him like a little girl. She did her best to sound humble. "I only wished to make sure that this man is getting better."

"And why would you want to do that?"

Marriam had stood up. Her back was to Peter now, and he could see her tremble. Hearing the terrible thunder of Wajahat-Ullah's voice, her warnings began to make sense. But his mind remained cloudy.

"I-I visit all the patients, Baba."

"Yet you sit by him. You talk to him as if he were a friend!"
She hesitated.

"I asked you a question," he shouted. It was a command.

"It was I who brought him here, Aga Jan," she answered,
collecting herself. Her tone was calm and humble. "He is our
guest. Surely, it is my responsibility to see that he is recovering
from his injuries."

"His people have brought death and destruction to our
land." Wajahat-Ullah paused. "And they killed your brother!
To defy your father is taking hospitality too far."

"He is a human being, Baba," said Marriam, gaining
courage.

Peter saw her back straighten. Thoughts and feelings roared
in his head. They were ignoring him completely. He did not
need to understand what they were saying. A volcano of anger
and passion churned inside him.

"Yes – a human being who has no place in our land. Let
him stay where he belongs – let them leave us alone!" Wajahat-
Ullah spat out the words. "Go to your quarters now. If I see
you here again, I will not be responsible for my actions."

Marriam bowed her head. "Yes, Baba." She glanced at
Peter, giving a quick nod, as if trying to reassure him. Then
she turned and walked to the door, followed closely by her
father. The immediate danger was over.

Chapter Sixteen

03

One Tuesday morning, Claire woke up with a pounding headache. She took three painkillers and arrived at her office late once again, upending her supervisor's meticulous schedule. When she arrived, Cathy was standing in her cubicle, blocking her desk.

Cathy's treatment seemed increasingly unfair. Claire knew that she had always been one of the best workers in the word-processing pool. But she did not know that Cathy was getting pressure from irate bankers above her. In fact, Cathy was short-staffed, and counting on Claire to make up for it, giving her more and more work. But Claire was not delivering as she once had, and Cathy vented her frustrations by making Claire her scapegoat.

Now Cathy looked around to make sure the other workers were watching, then pointed at the wall clock.

"And what time is it, Claire?" she asked pointedly, including everyone in sight in the question.

"It's nine nineteen," answered Jill, who worked directly

across the aisle. When Claire glared at her, she looked away quickly and started straightening objects on her desk.

"Thank you, Jill. Did you hear that, Claire?"

"Of course." She was trying hard not to sound insolent.

"That makes you nineteen minutes late."

"I am so sorry. I came as fast as I could. I have a terrible headache..."

Cathy cut her off. "I have not the slightest interest in how you feel. My priority is to keep this office running smoothly. That is my job. Lateness cannot be tolerated."

"But..."

"I am docking you a week's pay." She looked pleased, as if the idea had just occurred to her.

Claire was shocked. "I'm sorry, Cathy," she said, raising her chin high. "But you can't just do that to me."

"Oh no?"

Claire's head throbbed. The anger could no longer be reined in. "Why don't you just fire me? I can't take any more of this anyway." It took all her strength not to quit – to leave herself without a source of income.

"Follow me," said Cathy, as if she was ordering a servant. "HR is just down the hall. You're nothing but trouble. It's not worth it."

Claire realized her mistake, but she could not let herself be humiliated by this woman any longer. "Fine," she said firmly, feeling stronger by the second.

With the guidance of a level-headed Human Resources manager, Claire and Cathy came to an understanding. Claire agreed to resign in exchange for two weeks' pay, saving Dunbar Patton the expense of covering worker's compensation if they fired her. During those two weeks, the company would tell people that she was not in the office, so future employers would not know that she had been dismissed. After that, they would simply say that she no longer worked there.

"You're a lucky woman," said Cathy as they left the office. "It's more than you deserve."

Claire turned and stared hard at Cathy. She could not imagine why the supervisor hated her so much. *This woman is sick*, she said to herself. She needed to leave now, before she said things she might really regret. Besides, there was nothing more to say.

She returned to her desk as quickly as possible, swept her few personal belongings into her purse and marched towards the door. Her eyes brimmed with tears of rage, and the door was hazy, but she managed a reasonable exit to the elevators. She was determined not to let her colleagues see her cry.

Thoughts crowded her head as she rode down in the elevator. The job had not been easy to come by. She had some savings. Maybe she could manage for a few months on her own. She had never asked for help from her parents, and she would not do so now. Her step-father would never let her mother give her money anyway. And her father was so out of touch and so far away.

As she stepped out onto the sidewalk, the tears began in earnest. She was scared, but she had no regrets about leaving the job. She looked at her watch. It was not even ten thirty. She walked quickly, and as the blocks disappeared behind her, rationality took over.

This is not such a huge deal, she told herself. *It happens to people all the time. I will figure it out.*

She stopped at a newsstand and bought a bunch of local

papers. The walk calmed her. It was only mid-day when she reached her apartment.

She hung up her coat and arranged the newspapers neatly on the coffee table. But she was yet not ready to open them. She was exhausted. All she could think of was sleep – after a good nap, maybe she would wake up and everything would be fine. The idea was a joke, she knew. But it was all she could think of to do.

Sleep turned out to be miles away. When she closed her eyes, the events of the day rushed at her again and again – surprise, anger, humiliation; her colleagues pretending not to look at her as she walked past them to the door. After two hours, she fell into a fitful slumber. When she opened her eyes again, her watch read 6:12 pm. PM? For a moment, she was completely disoriented. Then suddenly, she remembered everything.

She knew there would be no sleep that night. She took a shower and made a sandwich and a cup of coffee and watched the news on TV. Then she sat on the sofa and opened the newspapers, checking the classified listings.

She circled a few job offers, noting phone numbers and websites. Then she started researching on her computer. By early morning, she felt she had enough solid information to get going.

She made herself a big breakfast, then, with a burst of energy, started sending emails and making calls. Time flew, and soon she was surrounded by notes and contact information. She worked methodically without stopping, almost in a trance, determined to cover all the bases. The results were not encouraging, but she managed to find a few places which were interested in seeing her resumé. It felt like hope.

She was so engrossed in her work that she forgot to switch on her cell phone; in accordance with company policy, when she had entered the office, she had turned it off.

* * *

Since meeting Claire, Shahnawaz was a changed man. He was happier and healthier. The nightmares were gone, and thoughts of his past brought sadness, not trembling hands and difficulty breathing. He didn't dwell on his feelings for this wonderful woman, but he knew in his heart that she was the reason for his new interest in the future. He was having a hectic work week. But on Wednesday, with a few moments free, he could hardly wait to talk to her.

He dialed her work number, smiling. On her extension, a recording answered. "The person you have called is not available. Please try again later."

He frowned and pressed "end". An email popped up on his computer screen, and soon he was swept up in his work. By the time things settled down, it was after six. This time he tried Claire's cell, and got a similar answer, this one encouraging him to leave a message. Usually, she picked up right away.

For two days, he tried again and again, frustration, then worry, growing. He considered showing up at Claire's apartment, but didn't have the courage. It seemed disrespectful to invade her privacy.

By Friday, his hesitations were eclipsed by fear that something terrible had happened. He waited until seven, making sure to leave Claire time to do errands and get home from work. The doorman, whom he often tipped generously, recognized him and let him in. By the time he reached the door to her apartment, he was convinced that she would not be there. He rang the buzzer anyway. To his relief the door opened, and Claire was standing in front of him. She was wearing black leggings and a soft oversized sweater. Her hair was pulled back in a ponytail. She wore no makeup, and there were circles under her eyes.

My God, thought Shahnawaz, *she is so beautiful.* When she saw him, she looked stunned, then broke into a smile like a burst of sunshine.

"Claire are you okay? Why haven't you been answering your phone? I've been calling and calling."

"Oh, Shahnawaz," she said, her brow wrinkling. "I'm so sorry. Come in."

Her laptop was open on the coffee table and there were newspapers everywhere. Half a sandwich lay unwrapped on top of the plastic bag it had been delivered in, next to a bag of chips and a cup of coffee, half full.

"I cannot tell you how many times I have rung you," he scolded, unable to stop himself.

"I'm sorry," she said again, "but I don't understand. My phone isn't dead. I've been making calls on it all day long."

"Not your land line; I do not have that number. I tried you at work, and I called your cell phone."

"Oh!" The cell was nowhere to be seen. "It must be here somewhere." She disappeared into the bedroom and returned, pawing through her handbag. After a few seconds, she held up the phone triumphantly. It was switched off.

"Oh dear," she said again, switching it on. It showed nineteen missed calls and seven voicemail messages.

"Damn," she said. "It must have been off since Tuesday."

"Tuesday? What is the matter, Claire? What's going on?"

She moved some papers off the couch and plumped up the cushions.

"Sit down, Shahnawaz. Please. Would you like some coffee?"

She wasn't quite ready for his questions.

"Thank you," he said, settling himself. "I would like that very much."

Claire stepped into the tiny kitchen and Shahnawaz picked up a newspaper. It was folded open to the classified ads, a number circled in pen. It wasn't hard to put two and two together.

She came back with two steaming mugs of coffee. He took one and looked up at her quizzically.

"Are you looking for a job?"

She hesitated for a moment, then cocked her head and shrugged her shoulders. "Yes. It looks like I am." She sat down in the armchair.

"Any success?" he asked, raising an eyebrow.

"I expect to have three interviews next week," she replied firmly. "I am very hopeful."

"That sounds good," he said politely. There was a pause. She looked at her coffee.

"In fact," he continued, "one of my managers is looking for an administrative assistant. I could talk to him, if you think you might be interested."

She did not look up. "Thank you, Shahnawaz, but I don't think so. I don't want you telling someone to give me a job."

"Of course, I understand. I will not interfere, I promise. At least let me give you his name and telephone number. Then you can talk to him about the job and see if it's right for you."

"That sounds all right." She wrote down the number. Shahnawaz felt that he had accomplished something.

"Listen, Claire. Let me take you to dinner. We will not even talk about this, I promise. We've both been working hard. You deserve a break. Perhaps I do too."

It was an irresistible offer and the dinner was lovely. Claire's mood lifted.

She started the next day with new resolve, contacting more companies, even setting up some tentative interviews. But the market was slow and the interviews fell through. It was unclear when she would get a job.

Reluctantly, she called Shahnawaz and asked him to mention her name to his manager.

* * *

So Claire found herself working for Paul Gregory, a top-level manager in Shahnawaz's firm. Gregory was young and intelligent. He did his job well, but he was notoriously difficult to work for.

The child of a young single mother, Paul had been brought up by his grandmother until he was four. When his mother took him back, her new husband treated him badly, and she did little to protect him. His grandmother loved him, but felt he belonged with his mother. A year later, she died, and he felt abandoned by her too.

Women had failed him. Now, Paul was an angry adult, and that anger found its target in the women around him. His previous assistant, Marjorie, had found his behavior intolerable. A divorced mother with two children, she was a good and responsible worker. But for Paul, that was not enough. He was rude and demanding, ordering her around, and threatening her for minor mistakes. He made sarcastic remarks about the way she dressed and the colour of her hair. She resigned in disgust, the third assistant he had had in a single year. Before she left, she told him why.

Claire knew none of this, of course. She enjoyed the job at the start. She liked organizing and supporting people, and she wanted to do well, both for herself and so Shahnawaz would not regret his offer. Paul Gregory seemed distant and formal, but she didn't care. She didn't realize that he was watching his behavior, concerned that something might come to Shahnawaz's attention and threaten his career.

In fact, Shahnawaz, true to his word, was keeping his distance. His office was on a different floor, and he was very busy. No one in the office was aware that he and Claire even knew each other.

Chapter Seventeen

❧

Peter was recovering from his injuries quickly, but he did his best to appear unwell, asking for a wheelchair if he needed to use the toilet, and feigning pain as he hauled himself into it. There was pain, of course, but it was tolerable. He felt he deserved it. His driver's death weighed heavily on him.

He was certain that once his captors knew he was strong enough to try an escape, they would guard him carefully. There was a narrow window of time for action. He feared that a US rescue mission would result in casualties on both sides. He feared for Marriam and her family. He did not want to risk anyone's life – except, perhaps, his own.

There was no possible way to escape from the infirmary itself, but the toilet had potential. It had a locked door and a small glass window. From the window, at an angle, he could see a slice of the compound. What he saw was not very encouraging; the place was like a fortress, its twelve-foot walls impossible to climb. The massive iron gates were always guarded. When an authorized vehicle arrived outside, the driver blew his horn three times and the guards slid open a peephole, then opened the gates.

He asked Dr. Assad for a pen and paper. The man had seemed sympathetic from the very start.

"Why do you need this?" the doctor replied, frowning slightly.

"Who knows if I will ever be released. I want to write to my family."

"You are doing well. You will be all right."

"You see me as an enemy," replied Peter, sounding dejected. It was not difficult. "Why did you bother to save me? You should have let me die." His eyes were brimming with tears.

Dr. Assad looked concerned. "Try to calm yourself. Malik Wajahat-Ullah is known as a fair and just leader. Have we not taken good care of you?"

He brought Peter a pen and a pad. "Write your letter if it comforts you," he said. "But I believe that there will be no need to send it."

"Thank you," said Peter. "It means a great deal to me."

He had hoped to draw a map of the compound. But he could not see enough from the window. Finally, he decided to write a note to Marriam. She had promised to help him escape, and though he hated to involve her, he realized could not do it on his own. Three days after her father's angry outburst, she had not returned to the surgery.

He needed to contact her. He selected a young guard who took the night shift. That very evening, Peter caught his eye and smiled. The man looked surprised, but gave a tentative smile in return. He had been taught deep respect for his elders, and this wounded American was clearly his senior.

But that was not enough. The important thing was to make a connection.

"What is your name?" Peter asked a few days later. The guard looked alarmed.

"Hassan," he replied, almost in a whisper.

"So you know English?"

"A little."

"That is good; I am sick of lying here day in and day out with no one to talk to."

"Yes."

"You must be tired working so late," Peter continued, smiling sympathetically. "You could sleep a little on that chair. I can hardly walk, you know. I am not going anywhere."

"I am fine," replied Hassan, standing up straighter. His Afghan pride would not let him compromise his duty.

"Of course," said Peter sheepishly. "I should have known."

Still, it was a beginning. Hassan was bored too, and improving his English might lead to opportunities in the future. Peter was astonished to learn that Hassan loved cars and had worked for the Americans for a while as a driver. Each evening, Peter engaged the young man, and they began to talk about trivial things – the difference between weather in New York and the climate of Kabul; Hassan's family; the merits of American football versus soccer. But time was running out. As soon as he felt Hassan relaxing, he started a conversation about Marriam.

"The lady who brought me here – she does not visit the patients anymore?"

"Oh no," said Hassan, shaking his head. "She is not allowed here."

It was no surprise to learn that she was forbidden to come to the surgery.

"Why? She was so kind to everyone."

"I do not know."

"Do you see her often?" Peter wanted to make sure she had not been sent away by her father.

"Of course. At eating time." Afghan tradition dictated that all members of a household eat together, helping themselves from communal dishes. Women served the food, then joined in.

"I would like to ask you a favor," said Peter, as if he were talking to a friend. "I can see that you are someone who can be trusted, and it would mean a great deal to me. He looked into Hassan's eyes. "Please give this note to that lady. I want to thank her for saving my life."

"Okay," said Hassan, putting the letter in his pocket. "But she is not allowed here." Hassan was young – he was not looking for hidden motives behind Peter's words.

For the first time since he had woken up in the compound, Peter let himself feel a glimmer of hope. He felt sure that Hassan would contact Marriam. And that Marriam would come.

Peter often dozed through the long afternoons. But the following day, he was wide awake. When Hassan came, the young man nodded at him, and Peter knew he had spoken to Marriam. There were only two other patients in the surgery now, and when they fell asleep, Hassan handed Peter a small piece of paper. The light was just enough for him to make out the words. His heart filled with strength just knowing that Marriam had written them. The next day, she wrote, she would come.

The anticipation of actually seeing her was a tonic in itself. He saw her the instant she appeared in the doorway. She stopped briefly to speak to the other patients, but he could hardly contain his joy.

"Hello Peter," she said, smiling a little. "How are you?"

"I am much better," he replied, beaming. "Now you are here, I am totally well." She smiled a little, but he knew she was serious.

"Well enough to travel?"

"Well enough to do whatever you tell me."

"We can talk today," she said. "My father is visiting another village. I intend to help you get out of here. Hassan will bring you clothing, so that you can blend with the people. There will be a turban also. If any one looks at you, you must cover your face with it."

He found it hard to listen as Marriam sketched out her plan. With each word, it became clearer to him that this escape would be the end of his journey of love. If he made it back to the barracks, all communication with Marriam would cease. He knew she would never reply to emails. He would never see her or talk to her again. He felt a tightness in his chest, as if his heart was getting smaller and smaller. Then, in a flash, the unbridled passion that had brought him to this place flooded through him. He could not live without her.

I will not leave, he thought wildly. *I will marry her and become one of the family. I will learn to please her father.* He knew it made no sense even as he thought it.

"I cannot bear to leave you, Marriam," he burst out. "Come with me. My garrison will protect us. We will be married."

"What?" Marriam's eyes were wide with shock and disbelief. "What are you saying?"

"Run away with me. Stay with me. We can be together."

"I thought you had recovered. But you are still unwell. I cannot listen to this madness. I must go." And with a look of despair and exasperation, she turned away from him.

"Wait, Marriam, don't go," he pleaded. "You are right. Of course you are right. I love you so much. I apologize."

"I know this is hard, Peter, but you must do what I say. I will give you one more chance. There is no time. Things are getting worse. My father has had no response on the release of prisoners. He walks a fine line between the Afghan government and the Taliban to keep his power and protect his people. He cares about tradition and honor. My wishes mean nothing compared to his duty and his life's work. You are a bargaining chip to him. He is thinking of selling you outright to the Taliban. They surely will kill you."

"Then I will die," said Peter.

As he said it, Marriam's father walked into the room. He had returned to the house to retrieve important documents for his meeting and had asked casually about Marriam. A servant said that she had seen her entering the surgery.

"What are you doing here Marriam?" he shouted in Pashto. "I told you to stay away from here. And why are you talking to this one man? Why are you so interested in him? I always find you beside this man's bed."

Marriam turned to face her father. She paused only a second.

"It is true, Baba. But this man is my responsibility."

"Your responsibility? Why? You speak as if you know him?"

"No...not really."

"I would like to speak with you, sir." It was Peter. Marriam

shot a furious glance at him. Her father looked at him for the
first time.

As usual, Marriam's presence had clouded Peter's judgment.
He was fed up with feeling helpless, with feigning illness.
His true sickness was love. Though he didn't understand the
words, the meaning of this exchange was clear. Whatever the
outcome, this, he was sure, would be his last chance to speak
to Marriam's father.

"You wish to speak to me?" said Wajahat-Ullah in English.
"First, tell me – do you know my daughter?" He glared at
Peter.

"Yes, sir, I have known her for some months now."

"That is not possible. You are lying."

"I am telling the truth. I am in charge of Allied security at
the school where she works. That is where I met her."

Marriam took a step back. Her face was pale, and Peter
could see her hand trembling.

"I was coming here to see her when the Taliban attacked
my troops."

"Coming here?" He turned to his daughter, still speaking
English. He took her chin in his hand and raised her head
so she was looking at him. "Coming to see you? Is that true
Marriam?" She steadied herself and looked into his eyes.

"I never encouraged him in any way, Baba. He was
patrolling and he saw a car hit a student. He brought her
into the school, then accompanied us to the hospital. It was
a few months ago. That is the only time we have ever spoken
to each other."

He turned to Peter again.

"Is she telling the truth?"

One of Wajahat's many strengths was his ability to judge

the character of those who came before him. He knew that Peter would not lie.

"Yes, sir, that is true. There has been no contact – not from Marriam." He hesitated only a moment. "But the real truth is that I love her. I am asking you for her hand in marriage."

Wajahat-Ullah frowned. His eyes blazed. "Love her? Marry her?" He spat out the words. "Are you mad? She cannot marry you. You are not even a Muslim."

"No. I am not a practising Christian either. But I believe in the same God as you do. And I believe in love."

"Enough," cried Wajahat-Ullah. "I will hear no more of this blasphemy." He took his daughter by the shoulder and turned her towards the door. "Go back to the house immediately, Marriam. I will talk to you later." Then he turned to Peter.

"I will lock you up the minute you can leave this bed."

"Please, sir," said Peter quietly. "I love her beyond all things. She is the world to me."

Wajahat-Ullah did not reply. He caught up with Marriam, held her arm and walked her to the door. She managed to glance back for a second, mouthing the words, "I will come."

Peter watched her go, then continued to stare at the doorway, as if the force of his will could make her reappear. For a few moments, he felt nothing, as if he were in a trance. Then reality hit him, almost like a physical blow. His outburst had endangered not only his own life, but Marriam's as well. Women were loved and respected in this tribal society, but they made no life choices on their own. They could not choose an education or career, much less a life partner. Such decisions were made by the men of the family. No Afghan would tolerate the things Peter had said to her father.

Now, he would be guarded day and night. He had slammed the door on his chance to escape with his own hands. He would never see her again, and he would never get home.

How could I be so stupid? Stupid! Selfish! Thoughtless! The words echoed like blows inside his head long into the night.

Indeed, his situation did change dramatically. A guard was specifically assigned to watch over him in the day, and another, new one, at night. They paced the floor or settled on the chair, never more than a few feet from his bed. Peter tried talking to them, but they never answered or acknowledged him in any way. He felt less than human.

At least they believe that I still cannot walk, he thought. *Otherwise, they would cuff me or tie me to the bed.*

He felt wrapped in a black cloud of misery. And then, a ray of hope. Hassan reappeared, with new duties. He brought food to the patients, and sometimes accompanied the doctors on their rounds. The first time he handed Peter a tray, he smiled. Peter managed to smile back. He was still a friend.

At lunchtime, however, Hassan seemed nervous. He was frowning as he placed the tray on Peter's lap, then gave him a meaningful look. "Destroy it," he whispered, and then he was gone.

Is he warning me not to eat the food? thought Peter. *Surely, they would not poison me.*

When he raised the cup of tea to his lips, he understood. A small piece of paper lay folded beneath it. Peter put down the cup immediately. And when the guard looked away for an instant, he hid the paper under his leg. After lunch, the guard began pacing up and down the room. As he walked toward the door, Peter managed to turn away from him and open the paper. It was a note from Marriam, written in tiny letters. It read:

Hassan will bring local clothing and show you how to wear it. My father is negotiating to sell you to the Sherwani Taliban. They boast of killing many unbelievers. You will not survive. You must leave before the deal goes through. More to come soon.

Peter managed to read the letter twice before shredding it into tiny pieces. Bit by bit, he managed to swallow them. It pained him to destroy words Marriam had written for him, but at least they were part of him now.

That night, when Hassan wheeled in the cart with the dinner trays, he was carrying a flat bundle under his arm. He lingered, coming in and out until the guard fell asleep on the chair. Then he handed the bundle to Peter.

"*Shalwar kameez,*" Hassan whispered – a long tunic, baggy pants, and a length of cloth for a turban, as Peter had learned when he first arrived in Afghanistan.

"Where can I put it?"

"Hide it," whispered Hassan. "We leave tomorrow night."

"We? Are you coming with me?"

"Yes. Miss Marriam also."

The guard stirred, and Hassan left immediately. There was no time for questions.

Peter's gloom shifted instantly to incandescent joy. Practical concerns vanished and magical thinking took over.

Marriam is coming, he thought again and again. *She will be with me. She loves me!* The thoughts got wilder and wilder. He even let himself think about a wedding. *My commander can marry us. Once we are married, we will be together forever. My*

parents will love her as I do. Back home, we will have a reception.
Everyone will come.

He flattened the bundle beneath him and slept and slept.

Chapter Eighteen

☙

At first, Claire liked working for Paul Gregory. He let her know what he needed, and she learned quickly to do an excellent job. She was determined to excel this time, to be professional and make Shahnawaz pleased with his decision to recommend her.

Paul was being careful too. Shahnawaz had made it clear that he disapproved of so many changes in the department, and Paul had no desire for his boss to dig deeper into their causes.

Claire was pleased that things were running smoothly and grateful to Shahnawaz for treating her the same as any other employee. She seldom saw him in the office, and when she did, he paid no special attention to her. During the week, they were merely colleagues. On weekends, however, they delighted in each other's company, keeping their relationship low key and enjoying simple pleasures – meals, movies, concerts, or a long drive in the country.

One Saturday morning, Shahnawaz called to say that he had work to finish, so he wouldn't be there until at least two. That was fine with Claire. She went back to sleep, woke slowly and took a luxurious bath. Then treated herself to a late breakfast of Earl Grey tea and an almond croissant. She had just enjoyed a final stray sliced almond, when the phone rang.

It was David Anderson. She was glad to reconnect with him. They had hardly spoken since they had both recovered from the disastrous ride home from the party, and their brief stay in the hospital.

"It's great to hear your voice, Claire. I've been meaning to call you. But not this way, I'm afraid. There's some scary news about Peter."

"Peter? Oh God, what's happened?" The instant she heard his name, she realized how little she had been thinking of him lately.

"He's been captured, and the Taliban are demanding the release of three prisoners in exchange for his freedom."

"That's terrible. How did you find out?"

"Peter's father called and asked me to come over. His mother is having a tough time with this."

"That poor woman. I should go and see them too."

"I thought so too – that's why I called you. We can go together if you like."

"Great idea – I haven't seen them for a long time. When are you planning to go?"

"Today is the only time I can do it for a while. Sorry to be so last minute, but I don't want to wait on this."

"Of course. It's important." They made a plan to meet in an hour near Peter's house. Then Claire rang Shahnawaz to put him off until late afternoon. She knew that it had been hard for him to carve out time to see her, but felt sure that he would be relieved to have the extra time to catch up on his work.

* * *

Peter's father answered the door, looking tired and distraught, clearly relieved to have some back up. He gave Claire a hug and slapped David on the back.

"Thank you both for coming so quickly. My wife could use some cheering up. I'm not so good at it right now, I'm afraid. She's in the den."

They climbed the stairs to the second floor. Mrs. Jenkins was sitting on the sofa, trying to read a newspaper. Her hair had hardly been combed, and her eyes were red with tears. She jumped up and gave both of them a hug, lingering with her arms around Claire. Then she stood back and looked at her for a moment.

"It's wonderful to see you Claire. You are so kind to come too."

"It's nothing," said Claire, feeling guilty for neglecting them. "I really wanted to."

Claire sat down with her on the sofa, and David perched in an armchair, leaning forward, full of concern, holding her hand. Peter's father hovered at the doorway, looking helpless.

"Don't worry, Mrs. Jenkins," said David. "This happens all the time. Our guys will figure it out. The Taliban don't stand a chance against them."

"You don't understand," said Mrs. Jenkins, her eyes filling with tears. "I'm scared for Peter, really scared. But I'm angry too. I know our troops have the advantage. But we've spent billions of dollars for years and years, and men keep on dying.

And we never seem to accomplish anything. Why is Peter even in this situation? What is he fighting for?"

"It's a crazy war," said Claire. "But what matters right now is Peter. He will come back safe and sound. I know it."

In fact, there was little anyone could say, but having Peter's friends there meant a lot to his parents. After spending a couple of hours with them, David and Claire even managed to make Mrs. Jenkins laugh a little. Both were glad to have gone.

They shared a cab home.

"Can I ask you a personal question, Claire?" said David.

"Why not," said Claire, anticipating the question and dreading it.

"You seem so together about what's going on with Peter. It's not really my business, but are you guys still engaged?" There was a moment of silence.

"I hope you don't mind my asking," he added.

Claire gave a sigh. Maybe it was good to talk about it a little after all.

"No, David, we've decided to give it a break." She paused. "You know, we were never officially engaged anyway."

"What happened?"

"Actually, I think he's in love with someone else."

"Wow," said David. "That's mind-blowing."

"No, it's all right. In fact, I've realized that I'm not really in love with him either. I still care about him, of course."

"I had no idea," said David. It was more than he wanted to get into right then. Claire was relieved when he changed the subject. At home, she took her shoes off and lay on the bed, thinking about Peter. Then she closed her eyes and fell into a deep sleep. She was exhausted.

* * *

It was late afternoon when Shahnawaz got to a stopping point in his work. He checked his phone and listened to Claire's message, then tried to call her. But her phone was switched off. He decided to wait for her to call him. They were going to a matinee on Sunday anyway. He was not comfortable enough to appear at her door without warning.

Claire woke early, still worrying about Peter. She waited till after breakfast, then rang Shahnawaz.

"Hello, Claire? I'm so glad to hear from you. I couldn't reach you last night."

"I'm sorry, Shahnawaz, I fell asleep really early. I don't think I'm really up for a play this afternoon. Would you be upset if I didn't go?"

"Is something the matter, Claire? You were not at home yesterday and today you do not feel like going out?"

"I was with Peter's parents."

"Peter's parents?" These days, Claire never mentioned Peter, to say nothing of his family. "What has happened? Is he all right?"

"I hope so. He's been captured."

"That is terrible. You must be very worried for him."

"I am. And there's nothing I can do, of course. It's hard."

"I will come to your place and cheer you up."

"That's fine, I guess. But I'm not really at my sunniest."

"That is why I am coming. I will be there soon." On the way over, Shahnawaz wondered about Claire's feelings for Peter, and for himself too.

When he arrived, he tried his best to reassure her.

"Peter will be okay, you know. He will come home safe and sound."

"I hope so. That's what I told his mother."

"So you are not in the mood for going out today?"

"Not really. Peter's parents are sick with worry: I keep seeing his mother's face in my mind. My heart went out to her. She was so sad."

"Of course." Shahnawaz paused. He wanted desperately to ask Claire about her situation with Peter, but he did not know how to begin. She offered him coffee, and he was relieved to have a few moments to collect himself.

He watched her graceful movements in the kitchen. She seemed herself. *She is even beautiful when she is making coffee,* he thought. *Perhaps she is not so distraught after all.* This gave him courage. When she brought the coffee, he held out his hand to her.

"Please sit down and talk to me, Claire. I want very much to ask you something."

"Of course," she said, taking his hand and settling next to him on the sofa.

"Are you still in love with Peter?" She sat back, cocked her head, and gave him a quizzical look.

"Why do you ask?"

Shahnawaz wanted to tell her that he was terrified that this crisis had rekindled her old love and eclipsed what she might feel for him. He wanted to tell her how much he loved her. But it was just too hard.

"I am here to cheer you up," he said. "But I would really like to know the depths of your feelings for this man."

Claire looked down at the floor for a moment, and then up into Shahnawaz's eyes.

"The truth is, Shahnawaz, I am no longer in love with Peter. I don't think I have been for a long time. We have been close friends forever, and we always will be. I care hugely about what happens to him. But love? I don't think either of us feel it anymore." She paused. "In fact, I think Peter is already in love with someone else."

"That is great," Shahnawaz burst out, unable to keep the joy from his voice. Claire frowned.

"What do you mean?"

"Nothing, nothing. I'm sorry. It just helps very much to know."

Claire wanted to know why, but Shahnawaz managed to change the subject. Talking to him made her feel better, as it so often did, and he persuaded her to come to the matinee after all. It was a welcome distraction.

* * *

In spite of his past reputation, Paul Gregory took great care to treat Claire properly. Claire herself preferred to take things at face value when she could, and did not waste her time analyzing her new boss's markedly distant behavior. Indeed, it was a relief to her. It allowed her to do her job.

But Paul needed to belittle others to feel powerful. It was only a matter of time before his real nature surfaced and the sham began to crumble. Sarcasm crept into his voice, and he became abrupt and overly critical of her work. The polite smile vanished.

Claire was bewildered by the change. She blamed herself, and made an even greater effort to please him. Paul in turn fed off her anxiety: it strengthened him to feel in control. Each day, he became ruder. As his behavior degenerated, Claire became increasingly uncomfortable. She wanted to talk to Shahnawaz, but she was determined not to bother him with petty things. So she ignored Paul's abrasive tone and got on with her work.

Paul had no idea that Claire feared disappointing herself and Shahnawaz, but he sensed her insecurities and fed off them, interpreting them as a positive response to his more forceful manner. He found that he enjoyed watching her as she sat at the computer, her hair cascading down her back, her slim ankles crossed beneath her desk. She was the most beautiful assistant he had ever had, and he wanted her to know he was the boss.

He started touching her whenever he got the chance, brushing her hand when she handed him a file, standing behind her chair and putting his hand on her shoulder. Claire did not know Paul's past history. She was astonished, but she did her best to hide her anger, pretending not to notice his advances, or, as they got bolder, pulling her hand away as quickly as possible, shrugging as if she needed to stretch, or standing up quickly, as if she had something important to do.

But as his intentions became unmistakable, she became more and more upset. She considered resigning, but she dreaded having to explain things to Shahnawaz. Besides, she had no proof.

The situation changed rapidly at a Friday evening farewell party for a colleague who was moving abroad. Everyone was drinking, and, after two lunchtime martinis, Paul was showing it. All pretenses were gone. He backed Claire into a corner, took her by the shoulders and spoke into her ear.

"It's time we took this to another level," he said. "My place or yours?"

"What?" said Claire, stepping back, horrified. "What did you say?"

"I want you, baby. Tonight." He leered and gave a wink.

"Come on, baby. Please." It was not a request – it was as if the outcome was certain. She took one look at his lecherous smile and slapped his face as hard as she could. It was a reflex, beyond her control.

"How dare you, you filthy bastard!" She was trembling with anger, astonished by what she had done – men had come on to her this way before, but she had never reacted violently.

Paul stepped back, stunned, holding his hand to his scarlet cheek.

People around them were staring, riveted to watch a live drama unfold.

"That's the end of your job, lady."

"Don't worry. Nothing would make me work for you."

It took a few seconds for Shahnawaz, deep in conversation on the other side of the room, to register that something extraordinary had happened. He made his way through the silent crowd to where Claire and Paul stood like two fighters at a standoff, scowling at each other. He turned to the other guests, who were standing and whispering, as if waiting for something more to happen.

"There is nothing here to look at, my friends," he said with a gracious smile. "Please, continue to enjoy our party." People started drifting off, and Shahnawaz turned to face Paul and Claire.

"What is going on here?" His voice was even deeper than usual, dark and very calm, like the prelude to a storm.

"This woman slapped me," Paul said, stepping forward as if he expected Shahnawaz to share his indignation.

"She slapped you? Why? She seems a reasonable person."

"She... overreacted," replied Paul, then stopped as he

registered the fury in his boss's eyes. Shahnawaz looked at Claire.

"Can you tell me what happened?'

"He grabbed me," she said. Her mouth was dry. In front of Shahnawaz, she could hardly speak.

"Oh? So you slapped him?"

"Yes, I did," she said, her voice breaking. She bowed her head. "It was totally inappropriate. I am so sorry."

"It is all right," said Shahnawaz softly. "He provoked you." He shot another black look at Paul.

"I'll see you in my office first thing Monday."

"Yes, sir," said Paul and left the room as fast as he could.

"Come with me," said Shahnawaz to Claire. "There are many decent people here. Try to enjoy the party."

As she stepped beside him, he put his hand protectively on her back, steering her gently across the room. People were back in groups talking now, almost as if nothing had happened. But it was more than she could manage.

"I'm sorry, but I need to go home," she said softly. Shahnawaz bent his head so no one would hear him.

"Wait a bit, Claire. I will take you home soon. I need another half an hour. After all, I am the host of this party."

"I'm fine, really. I can get home on my own." She looked longingly toward the door.

"Please Claire, don't go by yourself," said Shahnawaz, determined to keep her at the party. "Stay a little longer."

Somehow, he feared that if she left in anger, the relationship he had been building so carefully would be over.

"If it means that much to you, I'll stay," said Claire uncertainly. She felt as if she might cry. "Just give me a few minutes on my own."

"Thank you," said Shahnawaz. He smiled and squeezed her hand, and made his way back to the group of people he had been talking with earlier. After a moment's thought, he pulled Marjorie aside and asked her to check on Claire. She was known as a reliable and sympathetic person.

Claire went to the ladies' room and sat in a stall for a few minutes until she had collected herself. Then she splashed her face with cold water and checked her hair and fixed her makeup. Marjorie came in and washed her hands beside her.

"Are you all right?" she asked, catching Claire's eye in the mirror.

"Thanks. I think I'm okay now. "

"Come and sit with me," said Marjorie. "There's some things you should know."

Claire was surprised; she hardly knew this woman. But they settled comfortably in two armchairs near a huge glass window overlooking the harbor lights. Neither noticed the view.

"I'm so glad you had the courage to stand up to Paul," said Marjorie, smiling. "He's had it coming for a long time."

"A long time?" This was not what Claire had expected.

"I worked for him just before you got here – it was the worst month ever."

"Why?"

"He's great at his job, but terrible with people. He's bossy and rude. He comes on to women all the time. He's been through three assistants in two years. When the last one quit, I was assigned to him from the Pool: I was really relieved when you came along."

"Oh!" said Claire, thinking that perhaps she should not have kept so much to herself. She felt very relieved.

Soon, she was swapping stories about Paul's outrageous behavior. She even found herself laughing, and the shame she had felt for losing control in front of everyone faded.

Before Claire knew it, Shahnawaz appeared at her side. The guests were saying their good byes.

"Thank you, Marjorie," he said. "I hope you two enjoyed each other."

"I think so," she replied, getting up. "I certainly did. Take care, Claire," she said. "I'll see you soon." Claire got up and gave her a hug. "Thank you," she said, "it was great talking to you."

* * *

Claire was quiet as she and Shahnawaz waited for the valet to bring his car. But as they pulled out into the traffic, he could contain himself no longer.

"Would you please tell me what exactly happened in there? It's important that I know."

Now that they were alone, Claire felt drained and totally exhausted.

"It doesn't matter, I am leaving the firm anyway."

"Please do not say that. Give me the facts, and then we will decide what to do."

Claire did not answer.

"Please, Claire, tell me," Shahnawaz persisted, reaching out to her through the unfamiliar distance he felt between them. "What did he do?"

Claire sighed. He felt her rearranging herself in the seat beside him. "It was a lovely party. Really. I was enjoying myself. Then Paul came up to me and sort of pushed me into a corner. He'd been drinking. A lot." She paused. She could feel the tears filling her eyes.

"What happened then?"

"He said… he said he wanted to have sex with me. He said… his place or mine."

"And you slapped him?"

"Yes." She was crying silently now, horrified that she had lost control. "He was disgusting. I just couldn't help it."

"Of course," he said, stifling the anger he felt rising within him. "It was not your fault. The time has come for Paul to go."

"You don't have to fire him, really. I know he's an asset to your business. And I told you, I'm resigning anyway."

"No. It is Paul who is going, not you."

"I don't think I can stay with the company, Shahnawaz."

"Why, Claire? Why punish me and yourself, when the fault lies with Paul?"

"It doesn't seem right somehow."

"It is your decision, of course. I cannot force you to stay. But Paul is going in any case. Yours is not the first complaint I have had about him."

Claire was quiet as the BMW purred up the East River Drive, a line of glittering tail lights snaking in front of them.

"Really, Claire," said Shahnawaz finally, "there is no reason for you to go. Please come to my office on Monday, and I will assign you to Human Resources. They are short of staff."

"Thank you, Shahnawaz. I will think about it."

They pulled up to her apartment building, and as Claire reached for her purse in the back seat, he leapt from the car and hurried around to hold the door for her.

"Thank you," she said. She barely glanced at him.

He had hoped that she would invite him in, but she went directly into the building without even a goodbye.

He stood there for a few moments, aching to follow her upstairs, to comfort her, to declare his love, but he was reluctant to violate the privacy that seemed so important to her now. *Perhaps*, he thought, *a weekend's rest will lessen the hurt. On Monday, she will be in a better state of mind.* That left nothing for him to do but drive home. On the way, he turned the progress of their relationship over and over in his mind. It was difficult to keep his mind on the road.

Now that her engagement to Peter was over, he wanted to give her time to heal from that relationship, time to get to know him better, to understand his background, to learn about his values. Most of all, he wanted her to come to him freely, joyfully, of her own will. Then he wanted to marry her, to keep her safe and happy, to lavish her with all luxuries his money could buy.

He had been sure that they were moving in the right direction. But this evening, in the car, Claire seemed miles away from him. He was not even certain she would come into the office on Monday. He felt as if his careful campaign to win her heart had been in vain. Like a child, he blamed Paul for ruining everything. He hated Paul.

The weekend was a misery. He dreamt of his wife again for the first time in months. He tried to tell her that he had again found love. But she turned away from him sadly, and he was in darkness, alone. He picked up his phone to call Claire again and again, but each time, he cut the call off before the number went through. *What will I say?* he thought. *What can I say?* He felt he had lost her.

Chapter Nineteen

ॐ

The next day, Hassan slipped Peter another note from Marriam. *The outer door of the bathroom will be unlocked at eight o'clock tonight. Put on the clothes. Hassan and I will be in a jeep, waiting for you.*

Peter scanned the tiny letters a few times, then shredded the note and swallowed it. It was crucial to conceal the bundle of clothing, an instant giveaway that someone was helping him escape. They would question him, perhaps torture him to find out who. He felt sure that he would die rather than betray Marriam, but his mind was not so reliable these days, and he had no real idea how he might react to rough treatment. At the very least, he would be sent away, and Marriam's father might even order his execution to keep her from trying to find him.

The afternoon was interminable. When the wall clock read ten minutes to eight, Peter hid the clothes beneath his shirt and asked the guard for his wheel chair, feigning stomach cramps so that it would not be suspicious if he took longer than usual. He had managed to keep up the illusion that his pain remained so severe that he was hardly able to walk. He dragged himself onto the wheel chair. The guard pushed him to the bathroom and stationed himself outside the door.

He pushed himself up from the wheelchair with difficulty, and took tiny shuffling steps into the bathroom, shutting the door and locking it quietly after him. Then he stood straight and looked around the room. He had assessed it many times before. The door opening onto the courtyard had always been locked. Only the cleaners who came twice a day had the keys.

Peter changed into the *shalwar kameez* quickly. The turban was not so easy, but he had seen Afghan men tie them, and somehow he managed to twist it, wrap it around his head, and tuck it in. The mirror told him that the result was far from perfect, but passable. It would have to do.

From the small barred window, what he could see of the courtyard looked empty. He turned out the light and tried the handle on the outside door. It opened so easily that he almost pushed the door wide, but he managed to stop it, leaving only a crack. He could feel the adrenaline pumping through his body. His mouth was dry and his heart was pounding with fear and excitement. He opened the door a few inches and saw the beam of headlights in the driveway. He slipped outside and closed it, hugging the wall of the infirmary as long as he could. In the light of the moon, he made out a dark figure beckoning him, and he did his best to move quickly and silently across the compound towards the vehicle. It was difficult – lying in bed for so long had left him weak, and he still limped from his wounds. Freedom of movement felt strange and exhilarating. As he neared the jeep, Peter recognized Hassan holding a door open for him. With a sigh of relief, he climbed into the back and Hassan jumped into driver's seat. Beside him sat a small man whose face it was hard to see in the darkness. But no Marriam. Peter's heart sank.

"I said we would find a way to escape," said the man. Peter gasped, joy and relief flooding through him. It was Marriam, dressed in traditional male clothing just like his own. She turned to him and smiled for one glorious instant, then focused on the task at hand.

"Cover your face with your turban, Peter," she said quietly, doing the same herself. "Now, Hassan. Quickly."

Hassan started the jeep, barking a command in Pashto as they approached the gate, catching the guard in the headlights. Peter was astonished at Hassan's courage, and his ability to disguise his voice. The guard came towards them.

"Open," yelled Hassan. "Quickly! We cannot be late. Malik Sahib's orders."

The authority in his voice was unmistakable, and the guard turned back, pressed a button on the wall, and the iron gates swung open with agonizing slowness. The guard followed one gate as it moved, pushing on it as if to hurry its motion. It was almost two thirds open, when a shout came from the direction of the infirmary, followed by the sound of running feet.

"The gate, close the gate! The American is escaping."

Peter looked back, horrified that he had been discovered so quickly.

The guard tried for a moment to pull the gate shut, then turned and ran towards the button to reverse the movement. But Hassan floored the accelerator, and the vehicle plunged forward, clipping one side of the gate hard and knocking it askew. As they sped away, Peter could see it hanging at a precarious angle across the driveway. He prayed it would slow their pursuers down.

Hassan pumped the gas and the jeep picked up speed, careening around corners and lurching over the winding, bumpy road. Peter twisted himself in the back seat, watching the blackness behind them for a glint of headlights. But it was Hassan who saw them first, in the rear view mirror.

"There are two cars, Miss Marriam! Two!" His voice was familiar again, rising in fear as they plunged into the next valley.

"It does not matter. We must outrun them. They will turn back when we reach Kabul."

Hassan drove faster. Every turn brought blackness, and a few moments of hope. But then the glow of headlights appeared once more, closer and brighter each time.

On one relatively straight stretch, the cars came dangerously close. Peter could hear the sound of guns now – and as they rounded a bend, a bullet struck the side of the jeep at an angle, ricocheting off with a sickening *thwok*. The road was winding more now, the headlights revealing a terrain increasingly rocky and desolate.

After a mile or so, there was more gunfire, then a loud *thwock* as a bullet hit a tire. The jeep lurched and started wobbling drunkenly, losing speed.

Peter gathered all his strength. He felt responsible. Their lives were in his hands.

"We can't outrun them," he said, managing a certainty in his voice that he did not feel. "We have to jump at the next bend. On the count of three…"

He started counting as the jeep swerved crazily around a turn, and on *three*, they flung themselves into the darkness. Miraculously, the jeep continued on.

Peter lay on the rough ground in a daze, feeling sharp

pebbles beneath him. Everything seemed to be happening in slow motion.

He watched the jeep plough straight ahead as the road turned once more. It ground to a halt, then seesawed at the edge of an unseen ravine; slowly, slowly, it tilted forward, then pitched into the darkness. He could hear metal bouncing against rock – once, twice, then a scraping noise, the roar of a landslide, and a definitive crash, followed by an astonishingly loud explosion.

There was a moan beside him, and he reached out and felt a soft hand. It immediately grasped his own. "Shhh, my love," he said, "not a sound."

At that moment, the first of the pursuing cars appeared, followed closely by the second. Both flew by, their headlights carving a path just a foot from where Peter and Marriam lay, and screeched to a halt where the jeep had gone off the road. Four men leapt out and ran to the edge of the drop, their faces bizarrely illuminated by flames below.

They talked to each other and shook their heads. Peter could hear the gutteral rhythms of Pashto, but the men were too far away for him to distinguish words, even if he had understood them. He felt a large rock behind him and he tugged on Marriam's hand, half crawling, half dragging her around it. Her breathing was labored. The ground was incredibly cold.

"Be still," he said. "I love you."

He peered over the rock and saw the men climb back into the cars, back up and turn, heading for the compound. He curled his body around Marriam, protecting her as best he could, and heard her catch her breath. But the vehicles sped past in an instant, the drivers convinced that the accident had done their job for them.

"Miss Marriam? Mr. Peter?" Hassan was standing over them, outlined against the moon. "Thank God you are alive."

Peter felt something sticky and wet. There was a smell of blood.

"Are you hurt, Marriam?"

"A bullet hit me before we jumped. In my shoulder. It is nothing." The words came in bursts, as if it were hard for her to talk. "My father's men have turned back. You must go on – to Kabul. I cannot come. I will hinder your escape. Please go."

"I am not going anywhere," said Peter, unwrapping his turban. "We must stop the bleeding."

She groaned as he pressed the cloth against her back. Blood soaked it immediately.

"Go for help, Hassan," he shouted, though Hassan was standing right next to them.

"No, Hassan, do not go." She turned her face to Peter. He could just make out her features in the moonlight. "It is too dangerous. But you must go, Peter. Now. Please go."

"Hush, Marriam. I will never leave you." Hassan was still standing there. "Run, Hassan, run. Now!" It was an order.

"Wait," said Marriam. But Hassan was already gone.

"Now you go, Peter." She lay heavy in his arms, but her voice was fading, as if she were drifting away from him. "Go."

"Don't talk, my darling. Help is coming." He cradled her in his lap, pressing the cloth to her back, bending to press his lips to her forehead over and over.

* * *

It took Hassan twenty minutes at a run to cover the two miles to the compound. He started yelling as he approached, gasping to find the breath to make himself heard.

"Miss Marriam is hurt; open the gate. She is bleeding. Hurry, hurry!"

There was a barking of orders, and the gates opened, followed just a few minutes later by a scramble of activity and a small ambulance setting off. Hassan sat up front beside the driver; a doctor sat inside with Malik Wajahat himself.

As they rounded the last turn, the headlights caught Marriam lying in Peter's arms, still as a statue. Peter ducked his head and closed his eyes against the glare. Marriam's eyes were already closed. Smoke darker than the night still rose from the valley beyond.

All except the driver jumped out, and under the doctor's quiet guidance, they worked together as a team to ease Marriam onto a stretcher and into the ambulance.

Malik Wajahat climbed in next, and without a moment's hesitation, Peter jumped in beside him, folding Marriam's little hand between his own, willing life into her with his touch.

"And now you have killed my daughter?" said Malik Wajahat, his voice filled with loathing. "Where did you get those clothes?"

Peter ignored the question.

"Have them drive fast, sir, please. She has lost a lot of blood."

Five minutes later, they carried Marriam into the infirmary. She stirred at the bright lights and opened her eyes. She saw Peter at her side and managed to squeeze his hand. Then she saw her father too, his face stern, but his eyes bright with tears.

"*Bachay*," said Malik Wajahat. He had not called her that since she was a child.

"Forgive me, Baba," she said in Pashto. "I only wanted to save his life."

"Do not talk, *bachay*. We will make you well. Then we will talk."

"No, Baba," she said, her voice a wisp now. He leant closer to hear her. "I am… dying. Forgive me, Baba… please forgive me. Forgive Peter too." There was blood on her lips.

Malik Wajahat bent over and kissed his daughter's forehead.

"I grant you forgiveness, daughter," he said. "You have my promise." He stepped back as the operating room doors opened. But Peter followed in a daze, still holding onto Marriam.

"No," said the doctor, putting a restraining hand on Peter's shoulder. Peter stopped abruptly. Marriam was looking at him.

"Good bye, Peter," she said. "I love you."

"I love you too," Peter whispered and let go of her hand. The attendants carried the stretcher into the operating room, and the doors swung closed behind it.

Peter fell to his knees, rocking back and forth, tears streaming down his cheeks. He did not notice as Malik Wajahat strode off down the hall. No one paid him the least attention.

"Please God, don't let her die, don't let her die. I'm the one who should die." He had never prayed from his heart before.

"It is my fault," he continued. "My fault. Oh why did I come here?" He slumped to the floor now, talking to himself, awash in tears; he felt they would never stop. They soaked his shirt and streaked the floor, diluted by Marriam's blood.

* * *

Peter was still sitting outside the operating room an hour later, when the doctor came out. His white coat was splattered with blood, and he walked by as if the hallway were empty, taking off his mask as he went. Peter got to his feet and followed, standing at the doorway as the doctor approached Marriam's father, who was sitting in an armchair, his face blank of all expression. The doctor spoke in low tones, in Pashto, but his message was clear.

The tribal leader's face drained of color. He bent his head and put his hand to his brow. The doctor stood waiting for questions; but none came. After a few moments, Wajahat rose and strode swiftly past Peter, down the hallway and out into the courtyard without uttering a word.

The doctor stood there watching for a moment, then started to follow. Peter recognized him. He had tended Peter's own wounds in the infirmary. He stopped for a moment and spoke to Peter in English. Peter knew what he was saying, but the words sounded indistinct and far away. He held onto a carved pillar to keep himself from falling.

"I am sorry," the doctor said softly. "Her lung was punctured. There was much internal bleeding."

"No!" It was a cry from the heart. "She cannot be dead! She must be alive! Please, please, do something!"

"I am very sorry," the doctor said again. "There is nothing to be done."

* * *

Some time later, a soldier brought a chair, pulled Peter roughly to his feet, and sat him down, binding his hands awkwardly behind the back with a stiff nylon rope. Hours passed. The lights in the hallway dimmed. Peter's tears had stopped, replaced by a physical sensation of untold emptiness.

He dozed fitfully as the hours dragged by, until the pain in his arms became almost unbearable. Then, he heard someone talking softly to the guards at the end of the hall, and Hassan appeared.

"Thank God you are all right," said Peter.

"They will not harm me," said Hassan. "They do not know that I had been speaking with you. They believe that I cooperated out of loyalty to Miss Marriam. But I cannot help you now. Surely you will die."

"That is okay, Hassan. I am ready. But can you ask them to tie my hands in front? Please. It hurts so damn much."

"You have suffered enough," said Hassan. He went back down the hall and spoke to the guard for some time. *Maybe*, thought Peter, *he is asking for mercy.*

Finally, one of the guards brought some handcuffs and undid the rope. He stood for a few seconds while Peter straightened his aching arms and rubbed his wrists, feeling the blood rushing through them. Then the guard cuffed Peter's right wrist to the leg of the chair. Not long after, he again fell again into an uneasy sleep. He was awoken by the guards talking excitedly. Hassan was with them.

A few moments later, he approached Peter.

"They will go for the funeral prayers of Miss Marriam," Hassan said. "Then her body will be taken for burial." His eyes brimmed with tears.

"So soon?" said Peter, startled.

"The body must be buried as soon as the preparations are done. That is God's law."

"I must see her again, Hassan. I have to see her."

"I do not think so. Malik Sahib will not allow it."

"For the love of Marriam, Hassan." His voice rose with urgency. "Beg him. I must see her one last time."

"I will try, Mr. Peter. But there is little hope. Malik Sahib is very sad and angry. Miss Marriam was his only daughter."

"I know, Hassan. But please, please. You have done so much. This is the last I will ever ask."

"I have told you, Mr. Peter, I will try." Hassan left, shaking his head as he went. Peter felt as if there were a band around his chest, drawing tighter and tighter. His whole being was throbbing with grief. He wanted to cry, but the tears would not come. Once more, he found himself in prayer.

"Please God, let me see her face one last time. You have ripped her from me, but please, let me say goodbye."

He did not know what would happen after that. It did not matter. Without Marriam, he was nothing. He was ready, even eager, to die.

In less than an hour, Hassan returned.

"Malik Sahib is a compassionate man. You cannot join the burial procession, but after the funeral prayers, you may come for a few minutes to see Miss Marriam's face."

"Thank you, Hassan, thank you."

Peter closed his eyes while he waited, going over every moment he had spent with Marriam, hearing in his mind her final words to him again and again. *Goodbye, Peter. I love you... I love you... I love you....*

Finally, two guards appeared, released him from the chair and cuffed his wrists in front of him. They brought him to Marriam's body, laid out on a low bier draped with a fine rug intricately woven with red and green flowers. But Peter saw only Marriam, lovely as ever, wrapped tenderly in soft white cloth which framed the golden skin of her face. Her eyes were closed. He tried to imagine them open, looking into his own.

Suddenly his legs gave way, and he found himself kneeling beside her.

"Oh Marriam," he whispered, talking as if she could hear him. "Forgive me, forgive me for coming here. But I could not stay away. I love you so much. I miss you so much."

The tears started to flow once more. In spite of the cuffs, he managed to wipe them on his sleeve. He took a deep breath to calm himself. He did not want to make a scene with the guards watching.

"Don't be lonely, my darling," he whispered. "I am coming. I will be with you soon."

After a few minutes, the guards pulled him to his feet.

"No, please, I cannot leave her," he said, looking wildly around. Malik Wajahat stood a few feet away, looking directly at him.

"Please, sir. Let me come to the grave. I beg you."

Malik Wajahat ignored him.

"Take him away," he commanded, and the guards gripped Peter's elbows and propelled him back to the infirmary, where they cuffed him to the chair again and left him, miserable and alone.

* * *

Finally, light seeped in from the end of the corridor. The sun was rising. But the sounds of activity that usually greeted the day were absent. Except for a few guards, the entire compound had gone to Marriam's burial.

After some time, Peter could hear people returning. Hassan

appeared and uncuffed him. The young man's eyes were red and swollen.

"Malik Wajahat has summoned you," he said, and then was silent. Peter had nothing to say anyway; he felt as if he were being taken to an expected judgment that he deeply deserved.

As they approached the big house, Peter noted the cold blankness of its walls; their austerity matched the blankness he felt within.

An attendant opened the great door as they approached, revealing an unexpected world that melded luxury and ancient tradition. It took Peter's breath away.

In the center of the towering entrance hall stood a dark round table, and on it, a huge silver vase spilling with flowers. Majestic hunting trophies adorned the walls: at either side, two species of ibex: the horns of one made great sweeping arcs from the sides of its head; the other's curled straight upward in thick spirals over three feet tall. Facing the entrance, was a magnificent leopard's head, its mouth open in a deadly roar. They walked past it, into a long corridor.

At the end, two carved wooden doors opened into Malik Wajahat's office, a large room lined with sofas and cushioned chairs. At the far end, behind a huge mahogany writing table, sat Marriam's father. As Hassan escorted Peter towards him, the older man's eyes burned into his captive, jarring him back to the present.

"Release him," said Malik Wajahat in English, studying Peter's ravaged face. Hassan unlocked the handcuffs, and Peter rubbed his burning wrist automatically, doing his best to meet the older man's gaze.

"Sit," said Wajahat, and Peter took a chair opposite him,

straightening his aching back, readying himself for the order of execution.

Peter spoke before the sentence came. He wanted to make sure that Marriam's father understood.

"Sir, please listen to me. I have to tell you that your daughter had nothing to do with my coming here. It was my fault, my crazy selfishness. She never encouraged me at all."

"Are you lecturing me about my daughter?" Wajahat said, his frown deepening. Peter could hear the anger in his voice. "You need tell me nothing. I know my daughter."

"Yes sir," said Peter. He bowed his head. There was a long pause.

"You are free to go. After breakfast, my men will take you to Kabul."

Peter looked up; he could not believe his ears. "Excuse me, sir?"

"I said that you are no longer a prisoner," Wajahat said slowly, as if talking to someone hard of hearing. "After breakfast, you must go."

"No, sir. I am not going anywhere," said Peter, his voice trembling. "Kill me. I am ready to die."

"I said leave my house," Wajahat shouted, leaning forward and slapping his palm on the table before him.

Hassan took Peter's arm, trying to pull him to his feet.

"We must go, Mr. Peter." Peter pulled his arm away.

"No."

Wajahat's eyes blazed open.

"Go now, before I change my mind. I would love to see you dead."

"But, sir," gasped Peter, starting to sob. "I must die. I want to be with Marriam. I can't live without her."

Malik Wajahat leaned back as if collecting himself. He closed his eyes for a few seconds, then opened them again and looked deep into the face of the reckless young man before him. He spoke calmly now, his voice deep and implacable.

"I know that you loved my daughter, but that is over. She is gone. It is Allah's will. She defied my orders and tried to help you escape. The guards who followed did not know she was with you. She had always obeyed my every command. She loved me. But she loved you more." He paused again.

"You did not run when you could have. You stayed by her side to save her life. And she asked me to spare you. For these reasons, I am releasing you."

The dark eyes looked tired now, filled with sadness. He continued as if he were instructing a child.

"She could never marry you. It is forbidden. And yet she would never have forgotten you. I know my daughter. What happened is for the best. Allah is great." He laid his hands on the table. "You must go now."

"Now, Mr. Peter," said Hassan with unexpected authority. The command brought Peter back to his senses. He rose slowly from the chair, fighting the sadness that weighed him down, and returned Wajahat's steady gaze.

"You are a great man, sir. I understand now where Marriam's spirit came from. I thank you for my life. I will take the burden of your daughter's death with me, and keep her in my heart forever. I do not expect forgiveness, but I am deeply sorry."

"Goodbye," said Malik Wajahat. The words were final, as if closing a book. People were depending on him to lead them. This chapter of his life was over.

* * *

Hassan brought Peter to the dining room. He stood there in a daze, gazing at the long elegant table.

"I can't believe he didn't kill me," he said. Everything seemed unreal. He felt detached from himself, as if he were moving in slow motion.

"Malik Sahib is a truly honorable man," replied Hassan, pulling out a chair for him. "You must eat now – they will bring breakfast. I will make arrangements to take you to Kabul."

Peter sat down suddenly, no strength in his legs, exhausted from the physical and emotional toll of the last twenty four hours.

"Thank you, Hassan. Thank you for everything."

"Those we take into our homes are our guests. They are under our protection; it is the custom."

"We will drop you off at the edge of the Green Zone, and you will have to find your unit," Hassan continued. "It is not the most dangerous place. Still, you must not be recognized as a foreigner. Keep your turban over your face and your eyes down. They are too blue. They will give you away."

"There are many Taliban groups in this area – some our enemies; some our friends; some are neutral. But if they find you, they will own you, and there will be no more help from us. We do not interfere in each other's business. That is understood."

Hassan left Peter alone, and soon, servants laid out a feast before him – eggs with onions, tomatoes and peppers; sweet bread; soft white cheese with raisins, and steaming chai. He spooned it into his mouth mechanically, hardly noticing the flavors. But he ate a good deal. He was hungrier than he thought.

Chapter Twenty

CB

It was a beautiful cold Monday morning in Manhattan; a nice change after the rain. Shahnawaz stood at his window, contemplating the gleaming East River as it caught the sun, but the sight did nothing to lift his spirits. Would Claire come to the office today or not?

He deeply regretted having suggested that she contact Paul. He should have sent her directly to Human Resources, of course. He had heard that Paul had problems dealing with subordinates, but the behavior his manager had displayed with Claire was outrageously inappropriate. Shahnawaz was horrified that one of his employees would go so far. He did not let himself think that his reaction might be magnified by his feelings for this particular employee.

Five miles uptown, Claire was indeed hesitating to go into work, humiliated by the situation and the scene she had made. But after thinking it over again and again, she had managed to bring it into perspective.

It was Paul's fault, after all. Why should I resign? That's just a cop out, she thought and decided to go.

She dressed carefully, and when she looked in the mirror, a woman of sophistication and confidence met her gaze. *Image and attitude,* she thought. *Formidable weapons.* Being female gave her so many options on how to present herself. She was glad to be a woman. Men didn't have such choices these days – she thought of Native American warriors decked in war paint and feathers, and tried to imagine Paul that way, readying himself for battle. The idea made her smile. *What an idiot,* she thought, reached for her coat and headed to the office.

* * *

Paul arrived at Shahnawaz's office at ten minutes to nine, secure in the knowledge that Claire was planning to resign. He had prepared a diplomatic speech for his boss, apologizing briefly, skirting details of the incident while subtly laying the blame on Claire, and emphasizing his importance to the company and his ideas for its immediate future. After all, it was a question not of behavior, but value added. This was a business, and he was a prized asset.

Shahnawaz's executive assistant recognized him immediately.

"Just a minute, Mr. Gregory," she said. "I'll tell Mr. Khan you're here." She walked into the office, where Paul could see Shahnawaz absorbed in his computer. He noticed a frown cross his boss's face as the assistant spoke, and wondered briefly if this was not going to be as easy as he had assumed. A second later, she was ushering him in.

"Yes?" said Shahnawaz curtly as he entered. The look on his face was far darker than Paul had expected.

"My assistant has your termination papers. Please go to your office now and collect your personal belongings. Security has already confiscated your computer. I expect you out of here by noon at the latest."

Paul was blindsided.

"Just a minute, sir, please. Surely we should rethink this. What about the…"

Shahnawaz cut him off, his voice deep and definitive.

"This is the end, Paul. There is nothing to discuss. Your behavior has been totally unworthy of this firm. Stop in at HR on the way out. They'll make arrangements for your severance." He paused for a moment and looked deep into Paul's startled eyes.

"I never want to see your filthy face again."

Paul felt anger rising inside him, but managed to curb his tongue. He turned on his heel and left, grabbing his papers and striding past Shahnawaz's assistant without noticing the look of satisfaction on her face. There was nothing else he could do.

* * *

Claire arrived at the office a few minutes late. To her surprise, the receptionist told her to go directly to Shahnawaz's office; his assistant had her go right in.

He looked up as she entered.

"I'm so glad you decided to come," he said, rising and coming around the desk towards her, smiling broadly. "I've been waiting for you."

Claire had never been on Shahnawaz's own territory before. The size of his office astonished her. On one side was a low sofa of a rich grey felt flanked by two grey armchairs and a glass coffee table with an elegant asymmetrical arrangement of pebbles and flowers. Nearby, doors opened into the conference room, with its eighteen chairs and smooth rosewood table. On the other side of the office sat an austere and elegant desk of heavy glass with a neat stack of papers, a laptop and a phone, the wires artfully concealed by the legs and the carpet. Outside the window lay New York Harbor in all its magnificence.

"This is amazing," she said, forgetting to be formal for a moment.

"Come and have a look," he replied. He stepped back slightly, spreading his arms as if inviting Claire to take in the panorama. She approached the glass wall, mesmerized. Tiny gulls wheeled below, and the Statue of Liberty raised her torch in the distance. She thought immediately of the wonderful afternoon she and Shahnawaz had spent there together. She turned and smiled at him apologetically.

"I'm sorry," she said. "I'm not being very business-like, I'm afraid. I didn't come here to admire the view."

"It's quite all right," said Shahnawaz graciously. "Come and sit down, Claire, please."

She made her way across the room and sat rather stiffly on the edge of the great sofa.

"Just a minute," he continued, striding over to his desk. "I will tell Janet to call Human Resources, and we'll get you a form to sign so you can start working right away."

Claire cocked her head and looked at him questioningly.

"Thank you, Shahnawaz. But are you sure that's a good idea? It might be better for me to get a job somewhere else."

"Why, Claire? Don't you want to work here? Please tell me if you have reservations. I will do my best to resolve them."

"I don't mean to be difficult. But I worry that you feel an obligation to hire me. That doesn't seem right somehow."

"Nonsense," said Shahnawaz said forcefully. "This is not a favor. The timing is right. Human Resources is short of staff, and they have asked me for three new people. You will be the first, and, believe me, they will be delighted to have you."

He had never had to persuade anyone to work for him before – but he needed Claire to say yes. But he needed to be near her, and he was convinced that if she refused today, they would drift apart and he might lose her forever.

"What about Paul?" Claire asked.

"Paul is no longer employed here. He is already gone. There was no question."

"Oh dear," said Claire. "I knew you would fire him."

"Surely, you don't feel sorry for that lowlife," said Shahnawaz, astonished.

"No, no. He's rude and obnoxious. But he lost his job because I made a scene, and I don't want to be responsible for that. I watched him work and I know he brought a lot of value to the company."

"Paul leaving is in no way your fault, Claire. This was my decision. There were complaints about him before, and I had considered letting him go. This incident just confirmed the worst. The firm is better off without him."

Claire had nothing to say, so she kept quiet.

"So," said Shahnawaz eagerly. "It's decided then. Shall I have Janet call HR?"

"Why not?" said Claire, shrugging her shoulders and rewarding him with a smile. "Go ahead, please. Call them."

* * *

The job with Human Resources was fine. But after her initial delight at being near him, Claire did not feel comfortable with Shahnawaz as she had before. She bent over backwards to avoid taking advantage of her situation, acting reserved and distant when she saw him; he in turn became increasingly worried about the situation, and overly cautious and guarded in his approach. Their joyous, easy friendship was replaced by an unseen barrier. A proper employer-employee relationship emerged. Claire no longer called to say hello, and after a single rejection, Shahnawaz no longer called to ask her out to dinner.

Shahnawaz felt himself drawn back into misery. For a few golden moments, Claire had shined her light into his darkness. But now, that light had dimmed, and he had no idea why. He turned the situation over and over in his mind, trying to decide what to do. If she no longer cared for him, if his destiny was to be without love, he would accept that and leave her alone. But he had to know for sure.

He determined to call her one last time and talk to her frankly, no matter what the consequences.

Chapter Twenty-One

⁓

For the first time since Marriam brought him to her father's house, Peter ate without the watchful eyes of a guard. But he hardly tasted the food – the feeling of freedom that should have been so sweet was deadened by sadness.

After breakfast, Hassan returned and escorted Peter to a car. As a safety precaution, Peter was seated in the back, between Hassan and another man. They drove for nearly half an hour, stopping just inside the city of Kabul.

"This is the Green Zone," said Hassan, "but it is not safe. It is best to keep your eyes down," said Hassan.

"What?" said Peter. He had no idea what Hassan was talking about; all he could think of was Marriam.

"I told you not to look directly at any stranger, do you remember?" said Hassan with some urgency.

"Yes," said Peter, doing his best to focus. "My eyes would give me away."

"The clothes are Afghan, but your eyes are too blue – very American."

"Don't worry, I'll be careful." In his mind, Peter saw Marriam's eyes, pale green, circled in black, lovely.

"We are not far from the base," said Hassan, pointing the direction.

"Thank you, Hassan," said Peter, embracing him. "I owe you my life. And tell Sahib Malik I will always be grateful. He is a compassionate man."

"Allah be with you," said Hassan, and climbed back into the car. "Goodbye," said Peter and started walking.

The streets were familiar, but he had never encountered them on foot. He noticed words painted on walls. Religious slogans? He wondered what they said. He concentrated hard, walking cautiously, but feigning confidence, to keep from drawing attention. Men passed by; a street vendor with bananas called out, but Peter ignored him. No one really noticed him at all.

When he spotted the Army base, a feeling of excitement welled up in him for the first time, and he quickened his pace. He was eager to be back in a world he knew.

"Stop! Don't move!" barked a voice, and he stopped in his tracks, looking up for the first time. A guard was pointing a rifle directly at him.

Slowly, he raised his hands. He had forgotten his Afghan clothing.

"Don't shoot, I'm American. I'm not armed."

"Identify yourself."

Peter barked out his name, rank and serial number.

"Keep those hands in the air, soldier. You don't look like no GI to me."

He sounded an alarm and the whole area was suddenly alive with activity. Within moments, Peter was surrounded by soldiers. They frisked him, and he untied his turban so they could see that nothing was concealed in it. Then they escorted him inside, and a few minutes later he found himself sitting in front of his commanding officer.

"Welcome back, Captain," said Colonel Fredericks with a smile. "We didn't expect to see you so soon. Last I heard, you were walled up in the compound of some bigwig tribal leader. How did you get here anyway?"

Peter told the outlines of his story – how he was attacked on the road and left for dead, how he woke up in Malik Wajahat's compound, and how they treated his wounds.

"This Wajahat had been demanding the release of three men in exchange for your freedom." The colonel said.

"Yes, sir. That's what I heard. I know the US policy on blackmail, and I was worried there'd be more casualties if the guys tried to rescue me, so I did everything I could to escape."

"So you escaped on your own?"

"Not exactly, sir. The place was heavily guarded. It was impossible to get out."

"Then how did you get here?"

Peter hesitated. "Well, sir," he said, his voice faltering. "That is a long story." The colonel gave him a long hard look.

"No doubt you are exhausted, Captain. Take a break. Take a shower. Put your feet up. We will talk later."

* * *

It took Peter a few seconds to figure out where he was when an aide came to wake him up. He had no idea how long he had slept.

"It is 1900 hours, sir; the Colonel would like you to join him at his dinner, sir."

"Thank you, Corporal. I'll be right there."

As Peter dressed for dinner, he thought about what he would tell his superiors. He wanted to avoid his feelings for Marriam – or how he had felt driven to see her. He was determined to protect her name, out of love for her and respect for her father. Still, he would have to tell them something. He settled on avoidance strategy – no lies, but not the full truth.

In the dining hall, a flurry of cheers greeted him, and he was surrounded by smiles and well-wishers. At the Colonel's table, he managed to field the questions with short answers and a tight smile, eating mostly in silence. After dinner, the Colonel took him aside for a cup of coffee.

"You seem more relaxed now, Captain," Colonel Fredericks said, leaning forward intently. "But there are still a lot of questions. Are you ready for some now, or would you prefer to wait till morning?"

"I'm fine, sir. Fire away."

At first, the story spilled out easily without no mention of personal feelings. He explained that he had met Malik Wajahat's daughter briefly at the girl's school where his unit provided security, and that she had driven by after his jeep was attacked, and had her driver stop to help him.

"She didn't even know who I was, sir. But she had a big heart. I was out cold when they took me in, and they cared for me and treated me like a guest – it's one of those Afghan traditions. I'd lost a lot of blood. But later, she came to the infirmary and told me that I was being handed over to a radical group for money and my life was on the line. I couldn't believe it when she offered to help me get back to base. I went along with her because I figured that inside help was my only chance. She got me out of the infirmary okay, but Wajahat's men found I was gone, and they followed us."

"They didn't know she was in the car," he continued. He paused to make sure his voice stayed steady. "Then she got shot. And the old man released me."

Peter stopped. He found himself gritting his teeth. He felt he had been talking for a long time.

"Why exactly did he release you? I'm missing the logic here, Jenkins; it just doesn't add up."

"When they brought her back to the compound for treatment, she asked her father to forgive her for helping me. And she asked him to let me go too." He paused again. "And then she died, sir. The girl died."

"Incredible. These people can lie to your face, but they do have a code of honor. You have to give them that."

"Yes, sir. More than honor," said Peter passionately. "Malik Wajahat has tough decisions to make. A lot of people depend on him. But he is a man of his word."

The commander paused. He had not expected this man to come to a spirited defense of his captor. Clearly, there was trauma involved and many unanswered questions. These situations were complicated. A thorough debriefing and a psychological evaluation were in order.

"Thank you, Captain," he said. "For the moment, you will stay on base. You are exempt from active duty. Consider this down time – you've been through some rough stuff. That will be all for now."

* * *

It had taken all Peter's strength to sit through the interview calmly. Back in his room, all he could think about was

Marriam, her bravery and compassion, her beauty – and how much he loved her. But here, with his unit, he had to steel himself, to behave like an officer.

He managed to keep his composure through an extended debriefing by a panel of three officers. He answered their questions as candidly as possible, but managed to sidestep his feelings for Marriam. They were more interested in Malik Wajahat anyway, the compound and its security system, anything he had overheard. Peter told them what he could, but in truth, he knew little about what went on outside the infirmary. A week later, they submitted a report to the Colonel.

Peter's sessions with the psychologist were not so easy – the doctor delved into his personal life, his past, the explosion on his last tour that had cost his friend Paul his legs, and how he felt about his experiences in Afghanistan and the Afghan people in general. The psychologist was friendly, even warm. It became harder and harder not to mention Marriam. In their final session, the doctor told Peter gently that he felt that he had been holding things back. A few minutes later, he asked if Peter had any regrets. Peter sat without saying anything for almost five minutes. Then, he began to cry.

* * *

The psychologist's final report concluded that Peter was suffering from depression and PTSD – Post Traumatic Stress Disorder; continuing duty in Afghanistan might result in a total breakdown. He was to be returned States-side immediately.

Peter accepted the decision with relief. He no longer felt worthy to be a leader. He knew he would never forget

Marriam. But the bleak Afghan landscape reminded him only of her absence, and each night brought dreams in which she floated towards him, arms outstretched, then was pulled away by an invisible force to vanish in darkness. Back home, maybe, he could get some perspective; back home, a life without her might emerge.

Chapter Twenty-Two

☙

On Saturday morning, Claire found herself contemplating the twists and turns of the last months – and how she could never in a million years have anticipated them – Peter, Shahnawaz, her career, and now, again, Peter. Peter's parents had called to tell her that he had been released, but she had not heard from them since. She thought of writing him an email, but since their agreement to end their relationship, she wasn't sure what to say. She didn't want to give him the wrong idea, or upset him in any way.

Uncertainty about what to say brought her back to Shahnawaz, where her musings so often led her. She spent a good deal of time these days trying to understand the growing distance between them – and what she could possibly do to fix it. She had set out to make sure that he felt no obligation to her, but she had never meant to push him away. Was that what was happening?

She was deep in thought when the phone rang. It was Peter's friend David Anderson, who had given the goodbye party with her. She was glad to hear from him; they hadn't talked in a while.

"Did you hear the news?"

"No! What news?"

"Peter is back."

"That's fantastic, David. His parents called and told me that he was safe – but I had no idea he was actually coming home. He wasn't supposed to be back for a year."

"Well, he's at his parents' house now, and I get the feeling he's in the States for a while. Things must have been really rough for him over there. Maybe they sent him here to get some rest."

"I am so happy he's okay," said Claire, then paused. "At least I hope he's okay."

"I'm going to go see him. You should come with me. I mean, if you want to, of course."

"Are you kidding? Of course I do. Call his parents and see when we can come over."

Claire was relieved. She wanted to see Peter very much – but not by herself. A visit with David seemed ideal. He called her back, and said that Mrs. Jenkins had been happy to hear from him and asked them to come over the following afternoon. They made arrangements to meet and go together on Sunday.

After she hung up, Claire went on thinking – this time, about new concerns – what had happened with the woman Peter had mentioned in his last emails? What had he gone through as a captive? Could he have been tortured? She wished she had stayed more in touch. Poor Peter. For the first time in a long time, she went to bed not thinking of Shahnawaz.

* * *

Claire spent Sunday shopping and doing her laundry. The day flew. At five, she was getting ready to leave for Peter's when the phone rang. *Maybe it's David*, she thought. *I hope it's still okay to go.*

But it was Shahnawaz. Her heart skipped a beat.

"How are you?" she asked politely.

"I am fine, thank you. Listen, Claire, I was wondering if you might like to have dinner with me tonight. We have not enjoyed each other's company in a long time."

"Oh dear. I am so sorry, Shahnawaz. I already have plans. I'm going to see Peter with David."

She was delighted that Shahnawaz had called, and she hated to say no. But she couldn't back out now that Peter and his parents were expecting them.

Shahnawaz paused before he spoke again.

"Peter?" he said, sounding suddenly reserved, as if he'd taken a step away from her. "I didn't realize that he had returned."

"Yes, he's here, at his parent's house."

"I'm very glad for you," he said. "And for him, of course. Perhaps we can meet another time." And he cut off the call.

Claire was horrified. She looked down at the phone in her hand as if it held an explanation for this strange behavior. *No goodbye?* she thought. *Wow. He's never rude. He must be angry. What have I done?*

* * *

Shahnawaz took a deep breath. His worst fears had come true. Now, he understood why Claire had been drifting away from him. Peter was on his way back, and she still had feelings for him. Fate was laughing at him. He had started to live and love again, but now, this love was lost too. His heart wept. There would be no more chances.

Still, Claire's happiness was what mattered most of all. *She will keep on working for me*, he thought, *and I will be able to keep an eye on her. But she will be my employee. And I will learn to accept that. I will ask her to introduce me to Peter once more, so I can give them my blessing. Then, I will learn to be alone.*

* * *

David came at six as promised, and Claire went with him to the Jenkins house with a heavy heart. She was concerned about Peter, of course – but at the same time, she could not forget how Shahnawaz had ended their phone call – and the change in his voice when she told him that Peter had returned.

Mrs. Jenkins opened the door. She looked worried, but she managed a welcoming smile. "Thank you so much for coming. We've been looking forward to seeing you," she said brightly, and brought them upstairs to the living room.

"How is he doing?" asked David.

"Well, he looks fine. A little tired maybe." She paused. "But he's not fine, not really."

"Do you know what his problem is?" said Claire.

"I'm afraid I don't. He doesn't talk much. And that's not like Peter, you know. He's sad and quiet. He watches TV. He sleeps a lot. But he paces up and down sometimes. I can hear him up in his bedroom." She paused. "And sometimes, he seems angry for no reason at all." She took a deep breath and smiled again. "But we don't need to dwell on all that. I'm so happy you came. I'm sure it will cheer him up. Have a seat – I'll go and tell him you're here." She disappeared up the stairs.

David sat down on the sofa. Claire walked over to the wide bay window that overlooking the garden.

"It's so cold and grey out there," she said. "It was always so beautiful."

After a few minutes, Peter appeared, limping slightly. The difference was immediately apparent. He looked thinner and older.

"Welcome home," Claire said, and went to give him a hug, but he stopped her with a squeeze of her shoulder. And when David grasped his hand and leaned forward for a friendly slap on the back, Peter drew back and sat down abruptly.

"Sorry, guys," he said. "I don't feel so touchy-feely right now."

"Hey Pete, you don't seem so thrilled to see us," said David, never one to mince words. "Aren't you glad to be back in the good old US of A?"

"Of course," said Peter flatly. "It's better to be home."

Peter's mother reappeared with coffee and homemade chocolate chip cookies. Peter picked one up and turned it over and over in his hands, ignoring a shower of crumbs that fell on his lap as he did so.

They made awkward conversation for about fifteen minutes. Peter didn't say much at all. All of a sudden, he shook his head rapidly, as if trying to shake off water.

"I'm sorry," he said. "I have to go now. I have a splitting headache." He got up abruptly and vanished up the stairs.

Mrs. Jenkins looked worried. "I'm sorry," she said. "It seems to be hard for him right now.

"So, what do you think?" she said, turning to Claire. "You used to know him better than anyone."

"You're right," said Claire, her eyes filling with tears. "He's in a lot of pain. Something's really bothering him. I'm not even sure we should have come."

"He doesn't even eat my cookies," said Mrs. Jenkins bleakly, as if this were the most troubling of all.

"He needs some serious help," said David.

"I know," said Mrs. Jenkins. "I think the army knows too. They've set up some kind of therapy for him. He's got an appointment to see someone next week. I think he'll go."

"I'm so glad," said Claire. "If he says anything about it, please let us know. I'm so sorry, Mrs. J, it must be very hard for you." She got up to give Mrs. Jenkins a hug.

The three of them walked downstairs together.

"I'm so grateful you came," said Mrs. Jenkins, "and I know that Peter is too. It might seem as if he doesn't want to see you, but friends mean a lot. Please come back soon."

"Stay in touch," said Claire, hugging her again. "And let us know if there's anything we can do."

* * *

"I wonder what really happened," said Claire in the cab back.

"I don't know. But he's changed, for sure. It's like all the articles on soldiers coming back with PTSD. He's not the only one. Maybe he'd open up to you."

"Me?" said Claire. The Peter she had seen today was not the Peter she could talk to.

"You're the one who knew him best. Maybe you could help him get past this damn war."

"I wish I could, David. But we're not that close anymore. I was getting emails, but they were short and he didn't say much. We drifted apart. Then we decided to put things on hold indefinitely. Basically, to call it off."

"Wow," said David. "I didn't know."

"It wasn't that anything went wrong, really. I think we just became different people."

"But you were together for so long." He gave a short laugh. "I guess this means I can't look forward to a bachelor party."

"I'll try to ask him what happened next time I see him, if he's up for that," he continued. "I'd really like to know the truth."

"He was such a cool guy."

"He was," said Claire. She stopped for a moment. "Besides, there is someone else in my life now."

"There is? That's great. But you could have told me. Who is he anyway?"

"Well, this is weird on many levels. But remember last Christmas, when Peter was home and we went out to dinner, and this Afghan man shared his table with us in the restaurant?"

"Sure. He had some crazy name – Shah…something. Didn't he come to the hospital to see you?"

"He did," said Claire, her cheeks reddening. Shahnawaz had been so sweet and so protective. She hadn't thought about day that in a long time.

"So when are you going to introduce him to your friends?"

"It's complicated," Claire said sadly. She didn't want people to meet him while things were so up in the air. Besides, she wasn't sure what Shahnawaz felt about her any more.

To her relief, David didn't pursue the subject.

Chapter Twenty-Three

☙

Shahnawaz gazed out over the river from his living room, melancholy closing in on him like a dank fog. He stared into the horizon as the sky turned pink, then purple, and the river became a ribbon of darkness. Watching the lights blink on, he wondered how many souls in this vibrant city felt as alone as he did. He thought of that day back home so long ago, when his family had been murdered and happiness and love had been extinguished forever. And then, his time with Claire – his heart opening again, and the astonishing joy, like sunshine illuminating his life once more. He would not trade it for anything. But now that her boyfriend was back, that fantasy was over. He loved Claire deeply, and he valued her happiness far more than his own. But the thought of lonely nights stretching out forever was almost unbearable. *I have been strong in the past*, he thought, *and I must be strong again now. I will live alone if I must, but I will not let it destroy me. I have built a successful business and I will make it even better. Work sustains me and my employees depend on me. That must be enough.*

Yet he yearned for someone to share it all.

* * *

Claire tossed and turned in her bed, revisiting the good years with Peter, the funny, brave, vibrant man whom she had, she thought, loved. Each time she tried to pin his dazzling smile in her mind, the vision faded, replaced by the ghost of a man she had seen this afternoon. It was hard to believe they were the same person. She felt anguished at what had happened to Peter, of course, but also anger at the circumstances that had kept them apart, and how much was beyond their control. She had almost married this man. But slowly, inexorably, this war that she could not relate to or understand had slowly stolen him from her, and from himself too. She wondered if Peter would ever know love.

She closed her eyes tighter, and all of a sudden, Shahnawaz swept into her consciousness like a wave, drowning thoughts of Peter entirely. She remembered the intensity of her feelings for this tall handsome Afghan from the very start; the electricity that ran through her even when he inadvertently brushed her hand. That thought led to the long passionate kiss they had shared so many months ago, then the feeling of his mouth on her neck, of his strong body pressed against her own. The memory was immediate and vivid; it took her breath away. She wanted him so much. She thought of the happy, quiet times that had followed, as they had just enjoyed each other, becoming the closest of friends. Even then, she felt, they had been trembling on the brink of love. But who were they now? He was the CEO of the firm where she worked; and she was an assistant in the Human Resources department.

She ran her hands over her breasts and down her belly. But the touch she needed was not her own.

* * *

Shahnawaz left for work late, tired, angry and sad – feelings he had once experienced often; feelings Claire had banished from his life. No more. It was time to focus on business. He was still in a bad mood as he entered the office. He passed Claire in the hallway, on the way to meet her friend Jennifer for a quick lunch.

"Good morning, Shahnawaz," she said with more warmth than usual, remembering her thoughts in the night. "Good morning," he replied brusquely, as if he hardly knew her. *What is the matter with me?* he thought. *I cannot let this affect me so much.* He kept himself from looking back and strode on towards his office.

* * *

After a few minutes wait, Claire and Jennifer slipped into a booth at the coffee shop. Jennifer had become good friend; Claire trusted her.

"Shahnawaz seemed weird today," said Claire, barely glancing at the menu. "He came in so late, he missed the staff meeting. And then he was almost rude to me. He's always so polite."

"The truth is, Claire, Shahnawaz can be kind of unpredictable," said Jennifer. "Everyone knows he's brilliant, of course, and a workaholic. And he'll do anything for the firm and the people who work here – as long as they are loyal to him. But he has his moods, too. And when he does, the best thing to do is to stay away from him. Don't worry, you'll learn." Jennifer paused. "I guess you haven't seen that side of him much. But he seemed to have changed for a while there – in May, I think – not long before you started. All of a sudden, he was upbeat all the time – almost like a different person."

After lunch, Jennifer went off to do an errand, and Claire headed back to the office, turning her friend's words over and over in her mind. Shahnawaz's change in behavior coincided with the time they started seeing each other.

My God, she thought, *could his moods have something to do with me? I'll never find out, though. We never really talk any more.*

She mulled over the awkwardness of the current situation. The job was important; she wanted to be professional, to make Shahnawaz proud. But suppressing her feelings for him seemed to be taking things entirely in the wrong direction. The thought was terrifying. *Maybe he thinks I don't really care for him. Or maybe he doesn't care for me the same way after all.*

She felt she had to know immediately. That her whole life depended on it.

It was cold. She perched on the edge of the fountain in front of the Plaza Hotel and pulled off her leather gloves, taking out her phone and hugging her coat around her. Buses rumbled; doormen blew their whistles; carriage horses lined up along 59th Street neighed softly, shifting from hoof to hoof. She took a deep breath and dialed Shahnawaz's cell phone. He answered almost immediately.

"Yes?"

"It's Claire, Shahnawaz."

"I know," he said curtly. "I recognize your number. What can I do for you?"

"I'm sorry to bother you. I know you're very busy. But could we possibly meet for coffee after work? There's something I need to talk to you about."

"Is everything all right?" he asked, his voice softening.

"I'm fine, really." She paused. "I just need to ask you something."

Shahnawaz glanced at his calendar.

"I have a meeting this afternoon with some buyers at the Plaza. Why don't we meet on the steps at five thirty."

Shahnawaz was waiting when she arrived, punctual as ever. He took her to a small nearby coffee house with dark wooden paneling. It had an intimate, peaceful feeling.

"I'll get us something," he said, beckoning a waiter. He ordered coffee and cookies. There was an awkward silence.

"Well," said Shahnawaz. "Here I am. Now, how can I help you?" Claire steeled herself. There was no reason to delay any longer.

"Shahnawaz, I know this is a weird question, but… Were you happy when we were spending all that time together? I really need to know."

Shahnawaz frowned and stared at his cup. "Don't ask me that, Claire. Please. It does not matter now that Peter is back again safe and sound."

"It matters to me," said Claire, her heart sinking.

"It is time for you to find happiness with him. You will work things out, and soon, I am sure, you will be married. When you see him, please give him my regards."

"Wait a minute, Shahnawaz," she said. She had to explain; he had to understand. "You've got it all wrong. Peter and I are not seeing each other. We decided that long before he came home. The love just wasn't there. We were drifting apart even before he went back to Afghanistan. Then a million things happened. He fell in love with this Afghan girl, and got captured, and she helped him escape. But she got killed doing it, and that destroyed him. He's totally different now – not the man I used to know at all. He is really depressed; he hardly talks. I don't think he can relate to anyone."

Shahnawaz was silent. He bent his head and rubbed his eyes.

"Don't look so sad, Shahnawaz, please. Does hearing this make you unhappy? I can't bear to make you unhappy. That's the last thing I want to do."

He raised his head and looked directly at her, his black eyes burning. "I am sorry for Peter. I know how he feels. When I first came here, after my family was killed, I was like Peter in many ways myself. But I had my work. That was all I had for ten years." He paused. "Then everything changed. Happiness came back into my life. Darling Claire. I met you."

"Shahnawaz," she said, reaching across the table and taking his hand. "Of course I care about Peter; I've known him forever. But the truth is, after you came and picked me up from the hospital, things were never the same between us. I couldn't think of him that way anymore; all I could think of was you."

Those words were just the beginning; once she had started to tell Shahnawaz her feelings, Claire opened her heart. She told him how she loved his smiles and his silences, his strength and his ability to calm her down.

"It's time to get out of here," he said. "Come with me now."

They paid the bill and walked outside. Dusk was falling over the city. Opposite the Plaza, the glass cube of the Apple store glowed from within. He took her hand, intertwining their fingers as if he would never let go. They walked across

59th Street and into Central Park. The light was fading. Worried looking tourists were on their way out. But the park was still full of life. Joggers with skin tight outfits and iPods ran along the park drives. Cyclists zoomed by, fast as cars.

Claire was thankful that she was wearing comfortable shoes. In heels, keeping up with the long strides of this tall man would have been difficult. They talked as they walked. And Shahnawaz had a lot to say.

He told her how, when he had met her, a light had entered his being, a light of hope he had thought would never shine again. He realized that he had been sleepwalking for years, since the terrible events in Afghanistan that had torn his family from him; that he had lost all joy; that all that kept him going was the determination to not let life's circumstances take him down.

Claire told him that she had been attracted to him the very first time they had met; about the joy she had felt when she ran into him near their offices; and how she yearned for them to become more than friends. She spoke of the magic of their first kiss; and something she had hardly admitted to herself – that she had felt relief when she and Peter had decided to go their separate ways – because of the way she felt about Shahnawaz.

They walked out of Central Park at 79th Street, and a red light stopped them at the corner. They looked at each other at the same moment, and each knew instantly what the other was thinking. They crossed 5th Avenue with sudden urgency and hailed a cab heading east. The moment the door closed they fell into each other's arms, kissing and kissing.

The taxi pulled up to the apartment on East End Avenue

and Shahnawaz fumbled for his wallet. They tumbled out of the cab laughing, almost running to the elevator. At this early evening hour, other tenants were coming home; the elevator was full of people. They squeezed hands each time the elevator slowed down to let passengers off. When the door closed behind the final couple, they were instantly again in each other's arms.

They stood for a few seconds just outside the apartment, gazing at each other. Inside the door, they dropped their coats and let them fall to the floor, then began unbuttoning and unzipping, pulling off clothes, out of breath, stumbling across the living room, until they lay naked on Shahnawaz's bed, pressing their bodies together, as if they could become one being. Then Shahnawaz pulled back, opened his eyes, and looked at Claire, as if trying to take in every millimeter of her. He ran his tongue over her eyes and her lips, her ears and neck and breasts. With each kiss, waves of pleasure radiated through her body, building and building until she was shuddering all over. She pulled him up and covered his face with soft kisses. Soon, it was his turn to shudder. They made love again and again, until they could no longer tell where one began and the other ended.

Then, limbs entwined, they fell asleep in each other's arms.

* * *

Later, they stood looking out over the river together, Shahnawaz behind Claire, gazing over her head, his arms enfolding her. She leaned back into him.

"I have looked out on this a thousand times," he said. "The beauty brought comfort to me. Sometimes. But it was cold. I always felt so alone."

She kissed him gently. "You will never be alone again," she promised.

"I have so much to share, my darling" he said. "I want to give you everything."

"That's wonderful, my love," she said. "But it doesn't matter. The fact is, all I need is you."

Chapter Twenty-Four

∝

Peter shifted on the chair in the hallway, anger growing inside him. He had been waiting half an hour and he was ready to leave. The door opened, and a tall black man wearing a sweatshirt with a bulldog on it came out, his expression totally blank. He glanced down at Peter. "The shrink can see you now," he said, and disappeared down the hall.

Peter went on in. The room was small – just a desk and a couple of chairs. There was a photo of a sunset – or maybe a sunrise – on the wall. The man got up from the desk and smiled. A scar ran across his face, interrupting one eyebrow. "I can't believe it, man," he said.

"Whoa," said Peter. "Luke?"

"Remember that day in the hospital?" Luke said. "I told you I'd make a new start, and here I am. Sit down, man. It's been a long time."

"A lifetime," said Peter.

"Want to tell me about it? I bet things have been rough.

Maybe it feels like your life is over. But really, man, it's just the beginning."

* * *

In early May, Claire and Shahnawaz were married, happier than either had ever imagined possible. David was there, and Mr. and Mrs. Jenkins. Peter did not attend.

The parks were bursting white dogwood and pink cherry blossoms, as miraculous and beautiful as their own delight. Wounds remained, but love was soothing them – love that flowed directly from the heart, growing with each day, filling them, unfettered by prejudice, religion or nationality. Love without borders.

*** THE END ***

Acknowledgements

༌

To my husband, Zahid, thank you, without whose support this book would not be possible. He has been the pillar of strength in my journey of writing.

My four children, Sabah, Salman, Faiza and Yasir, all of whom believed in me and kept this improbable project going. My daughter Faiza gave me the much needed push to write my second novel. My son Salman helped produce the first draft, gave depth to the protagonist Shahnawaz' personality and spent many hours to get the book in this form.

My daughter-in-law, Monica, who went out of her way to help me find a publisher and introduced me to AuthorsUpFront. I am very grateful to Manish Purohit and his entire team at AuthorsUpFront, who treated my manuscript with such affection and efficiency.

CPSIA information can be obtained at www.ICGtesting.com
Printed in the USA
LVOW07s1957080616

491761LV00007B/734/P